STOP AT NOTHING

STOP AT NOTHING

Douglas Rutherford

WALKER AND COMPANY
NEW YORK

First published in the United States of America
in 1983 by the Walker Publishing Company, Inc.

ISBN: 0-8027-5577-1

Library of Congress Catalog Card Number: 83-40041

Printed in the United States of America

10 9 8 7 6 5 4 3 2 1

ONE

I was in the fast lane, cruising down the M1 at 130 mph when the announcer interrupted the programme of music on my radio.

'Here is a news flash:

General Sir Richard Stewart, deputy chief of NATO forces in Europe, was abducted by terrorists this afternoon in Southern Italy. He had been visiting the NATO headquarters in Naples and had gone on to pay a private visit to the British war cemetery at Cassino when he was overpowered by armed men and driven away in a car. His four Italian guards were killed and his ADC is critically wounded in hospital. So far no group has claimed responsibility for the outrage.

The next work in this programme of music by Schubert is his A minor sonata. Schubert conceived the idea for . . .

I leaned forward and switched the radio off. I checked my driving mirror and the bridge ahead for possible police cars. The road surface was dry, the air clear but surprisingly cold for an evening in late May. London was still a hundred miles away and I had a dinner date with Sally.

She was still in Nico's Wine Bar when I turned up. I guessed that she had been on the point of moving on with a suave Saudi-Arabian who had taken the stool beside her. He faded out when I made it clear Sally was my girl — for that night anyway.

She forgave me after the first glass of Veuve Clicquot. We dined at Chez Solange. She was well thawed out by the end of a meal recommended personally by the chef. Oscar Peterson was playing at Ronnie Scott's Club so we went on there.

We emerged at 2 a.m. She said: 'Your place or mine?'

'Mine. I have a bottle of really old Calvados.'

She worked her fingers over my thigh as we drove home. In the end I forgot all about the Calvados.

5

It was about 4 a.m. and I must have dozed off when the 'phone rang. Sally had fastened her legs round me in a good imitation of a grannie knot.

She muttered: 'You should have taken the bloody thing off the hook.'

'Let it ring.'

Ring it did. After a couple of minutes I extricated myself from her clasp and reached for the receiver. A voice was barking 'Hello! Hello!' before I could get the thing to my ear.

'Richie!' I protested. 'For Christ's sake!'

'Don't tell me you were asleep, old pal.'

'What do you think? You know what time it is?'

'You can't kid me. I can smell her perfume on the 'phone.'

'What's all this in aid of?'

'I need your help, Pat. It's a mite urgent. Can you get round to my flat right away?'

'*Now*?'

'Yes.'

'What's the problem?'

'Uh — it's my glass eye. It's come out and I can't get it in again.'

'Get lost!'

I disconnected, dialled 4 and laid the receiver down on the bedside table. That would stop Richie or anyone else disturbing us.

Sally received me back to her bosom.

After a few minutes she said: 'What's the matter? Don't you fancy me anymore?'

It was true I had not been concentrating on her. Richie was not a practical joker. There were some things he held sacred. He would never have asked me to forsake a woman in bed unless he had an urgent problem. The excuse about his glass eye was ridiculous enough for me to realise it was a cover. He had not wanted to tell me the real reason over the 'phone.

'I'm sorry, Sally.' I moved her hand. 'I've got to get up.'

'Well, don't be too long.'

'No, I mean I've got to go. That was a friend of mine. He's in trouble.'

6

'My heart bleeds for him.'

'Seriously. It has to be urgent for him to ring me like that.' She hoisted herself up on one elbow, angry.

'You remind me of a doctor I knew. He was always on call. It was like sleeping in a telephone exchange.'

In a sense I was on call. As part of Richie's new set-up I had undertaken to be available at a few hours' notice. That was sometimes inconvenient, but the assignments he gave me were very lucrative.

I pressed the cradle down, got the dialling tone, composed Richie's number. He answered very quickly.

'Richie. I'll be round in about fifteen minutes.'

'Good man. Don't park too near the flat.'

I left Sally in bed, telling her to help herself to breakfast if I was not back in time. She took it philosophically, thumping the pillows and wrapping the sheet tightly round herself.

I dressed quickly, put what I'd need for a night or two into a small shoulder-bag and collected my passport from its drawer in the desk. With Richie you never knew.

He had moved into a new flat in Chelsea, between the King's and Fulham Roads. Its opulence reflected the profitability of his new venture. Shrewd as always, he had anticipated the recession and baled out of the quality automobile business. He had sold his collection of Rolls-Royces and Bentleys while prices were still high and moved into a line which was one of the few growth industries in the prevailing economic recession.

In a world where terrorism and extortion were flourishing, the business of kidnap and ransom — K & R to the trade — was very profitable. Richie was not the first to offer a service for the victims of kidnapping or important persons who felt they were at risk. The leaders in the field employed more than fifty operatives and had successfully negotiated the release of over sixty kidnap victims worldwide. Lloyd's of London, maintaining a reputation for insuring against any risk, had earned seventy-five million pounds in K & R premiums in the past three years. Sums of up to ten million pounds had been paid out in ransoms. Naturally, the premiums levied on

7

clients were enormous. But the underwriters usually reduced these by twenty per cent if the individual at risk contracted to use the services of such an organisation.

Richie had deliberately kept the organisation small. His service was very personal. He dealt with each case himself, calling in help as he needed it from his extensive contacts in both official and underground organisations.

In less than a year he had established a reputation with the multi-national companies and with government agencies which take an interest in the clandestine world of espionage, subversion and terrorism.

I was a more or less permanent member of his team. Ninety-five per cent of kidnappings occur when the victim is travelling by car, so my special qualifications as a security driver were particularly appropriate.

It was the dead hour of the night and I made good time from Hurlingham to Chelsea. As I drove through the empty streets I asked myself yet again: Why am I doing this? Forsaking sheer sheets and a buxom body, fleeing from the gentle life to embark on another of Richie's adventures. No satisfactory answer. It was years now since Juliet had left me. She it was who shattered the sparkling idyll I imagined was life. And when she ditched me she took my son too — with the full approval of English Justice. All she had left me was a jagged blade embedded in my spleen. Whenever I thought of them it twisted.

My right foot reacted on the throttle pedal, the Saab flung itself at a set of traffic lights as they blinked from amber to red.

I parked the Turbo, now a company car, a couple of hundred yards short of Richie's place. The sound of music and laughter floated down from an open window above me as I locked the car. The sky was still dark. I walked the short distance to Melton Square. There was illumination behind the entry-phone panel of numbers 37-41. I pushed the button beside the name R. Bryer. At the end of the Square an empty milk bottle, rocked by a careless foot, went tinkling down a flight of steps.

'Who is it?'

'Patrick.'

The door buzzed and I pushed it open. Obeying the sign warning residents and visitors to make sure it was properly closed, I waited till the automatic lock had clicked before pressing the bell to summon the lift. Luxury had oozed from the flats into the hall and stairway. The deep pile carpet had been recently fitted, the polished mahogany table looked like a genuine antique, the gladioli in the Chinese vase were fresh. When the lift doors opened they exhaled a whiff of discreet perfume.

Entering the flat I realised that Richie already had a visitor. A hat and coat were hanging on the hallstand. The smell of cigar smoke drifted out from the sitting-room.

Richie smiled and patted me on the shoulder.

'You got the message. Didn't want to say too much on the 'phone.'

'That's what I guessed. There had better be a good reason for hauling me out like this.'

'There is,' he said seriously.

Richie stood just over six feet tall in his hand-made buckskin shoes and was built like a back-row Rugby forward. He still had a military bearing, though he now allowed his wavy flaxen hair to grow more luxuriantly. His full moustache was brushed up at the corners of his mouth and his cheeks had never lost the tan acquired during his years as a soldier or mercenary in equatorial climates. His eyes were of a piercing blue and it was not easy to tell that one of them was of glass. There was a finger missing from one hand and I knew that under his casual but elegant clothes were at least three horrific battle scars. His attitude towards women was enthusiastic but uncommitted. Any female of experience could tell at a glance that he was fancy-free and intended to stay that way, but they invariably yielded to his confident, buccaneering charm.

He shepherded me into the sitting-room. The brandy bottle was out and a couple of balloon glasses stood on the low table. I had the immediate impression that these two had been talking for some hours.

Richie's other visitor had already stood up to meet me. He was about the same age and gave the same impression of a military background. He was dark and clean-shaven with alert but wary eyes and a depression in the flesh of his chin. He was wearing a well-tailored dark grey suit with a charcoal stripe and a Guards tie.

'This is Charles,' Richie introduced. 'Patrick Malone.'

'Charles — ?' I was waiting for the surname, but Richie gave me a wink from his good eye.

'Better for you not to know any more. Charles and I were in the same regiment eighteen years ago. He works for COBRA now — the Cabinet Office Briefing Room.'

Charles was giving me a long, measuring look. I stared back into his eyes, prepared to hold them for as long as he wanted.

'Yes, he does look a bit as if he'd had a rough night in a Hong Kong brothel,' Richie observed, interpreting Charles's expression. 'But he shows up better in daylight, in fact my woman friends keep telling me he's an attractive bastard.'

Charles lowered his eyes to tap ash from his cigar into an ashtray. Politeness rather than weakness.

'Patrick is a founder member of the firm.' Richie moved over beside his visitor and stood there contemplating me with analytical amusement. 'We did a few rough old jobs together before we set up the firm, so I know what he's made of.'

'You said he was a soldier.' Charles's eyes flickered at me briefly, noting the unsoldierly bearing.

'Yes, for a time. Patrick's too much of a maverick for army life.'

It was tactful of Richie to gloss over my army career. It had come to an abrupt end after an incident in Northern Ireland when my patrol "over-reacted" to an IRA ambush.

'I can't give you much *curriculum vitae* because I don't have it. He's Slough-Irish, mid-thirties as you can see, hale, fit and shooting for trouble. Don't be misled by the Judo black-belt impression. He's no culture slouch, speaks French, Italian, Spanish and stammers a few other lingos.'

'What is this, Richie? A slave market? You trying to

auction me?'

'No way, old Pat,' Richie said with an unexpected burst of affection. 'There's no money I'd sell you for.'

He turned again to Charles, who was watching me with a different kind of interest.

'Patrick's speciality is cars. He went from armoured cars to rallying and then did some very special driving for the Home Office. As you know, ninety-five per cent of kidnappings occur when the victim is travelling by car, so his special qualifications as a security driver are particularly valuable in our work.'

'Okay.' I moved past the COBRA man and picked up the *Standard* which lay on the coffee table. The late edition had a headline about the kidnapping in Italy. 'You can scrub the Debrett bit. Let's get down to cases.'

'Did you listen to the news this evening?'

I nodded, guessing already.

'Then you know that General Sir Richard Stewart has been kidnapped.'

'Yes. I heard it on my car radio. Deputy chief of NATO.'

'Deputy Supreme Allied Commander Europe,' Charles corrected me, not chiding me for a slight inaccuracy so much as making it clear that we must get our facts right. 'SACEUR is an American, of course. That's always been understood. We haven't had a British deputy for some time. Remarkable man, Stewart. Won a VC at the age of twenty-one. He was due to retire in a year. When he goes the Army will lose the last senior officer to have served in World War Two.'

I nodded again. Everyone who read the papers or watched television knew of General Sir Richard Stewart, KCMG, VC, DSO, MC. Probably the most charismatic war hero since the fabled Monty had disappeared from the scene.

Charles did not expect any comment on his brief eulogy. He sat down in the big armchair. With a nod Richie signalled me to make myself comfortable on the settee. He moved towards the drinks cabinet, leaving the field clear for Charles.

'I said Stewart was a remarkable man. The fact that he was a war hero has tended to mask his real qualities. He's also one of the best brains in the British Army — perhaps the best we've ever had. He happens to have a photographic memory. I mean that literally.'

Charles was gazing at me with embarrassing intensity. He spoke in clipped Eton and Sandhurst tones, letting his voice do the talking, avoiding body-language or facial quirks.

'It is a rather unfortunate coincidence that Stewart has held three key appointments in quick succession. Prior to being posted to Brussels he was Director of Military Operations here. Before that he was CINC North — I don't know how familiar you are with the NATO organisation?'

'Not too familiar,' I admitted.

'CINC North wears two hats. Under one of them he commands NATO's Northern Army Group. Under the other he is commander of British Forces in Germany, with his headquarters at Rheindahlen. The British, God bless 'em, are responsible for defending the anticipated Russian route through to Western Europe. So Stewart carries in his head full details of the agreed NATO response to a Soviet attack, including our intentions as regards escalation from conventional to nuclear weapons and the whole nuclear release procedure.'

Richie put a balloon brandy glass beside me and poured in a little Rémy-Martin VSOP. I glanced up and met his eye. I had been in the flat barely five minutes and I was already being briefed on what must be the biggest intelligence crisis since the flight of Burgess and MacLean.

'Is that why the Red Brigades kidnapped him?'

'We don't know yet if it was the Red Brigades, but we have to assume the worst. It may be the work of *Colonna Nuova*. These new people are tougher, more professional. They've been trained in Libya, probably by Russian experts. They'll represent their motives as political and social. "Enemy of the people, symbol of neo-colonial aggression, harbinger of the nuclear holocaust", and so on. But they'll soon realise how valuable his knowledge can be to them — and their foreign backers.'

'If he talks.'

12

'Oh, he'll talk — in the course of time.'

Charles inspected the tip of his cigar. It was dead. He laid it on the lip of the ashtray and cocked an eye at me.

'Perhaps you are thinking that a man who won the VC would be a hard nut to crack?'

There was no need for Charles to tell me that the kind of courage which wins medals in battle would be of little avail in a "people's prison".

'Judging by what I've seen of him he would not give way easily.'

'There are things you don't know and which I can't tell you,' Charles went on in his careful, unemotional voice. 'But I'm betraying no secrets when I tell you that the situation in Europe is very finely balanced. Anyone who reads the papers knows that the Russians currently enjoy a superiority in chemical and nuclear weapons. That situation may only last for another year or two, by which time the Americans will reach parity and surpass them. The danger is that the Soviets may be tempted to make a pre-emptive strike while they still have superiority.'

It was coming up to half-past four on a Tuesday morning. Apart from the late-home night-birds and early-morning workers, London lay sleeping all around us. And here I was on the third floor of a block of flats in Chelsea listening to a man from the Cabinet Office calmly talking about the prospects for World War Three. I picked up the glass Richie had thoughtfully provided and cupped its rounded bottom in my hand.

'We know that the Warsaw Pact countries are carrying out a massive exercise along the Polish frontier. They've done that before. Of course we have official observers watching it and our monitoring service at Cheltenham is listening to all their signals. But what worries us is that since yesterday a total wireless silence has been observed by all Russian units in the area opposite Northag — that's Northern Army Group.'

'Could be part of the exercise,' Richie suggested from behind Charles's chair.

'It could,' Charles agreed. 'I can't go into more details

13

without divulging information which you don't need to know. I'm only touching on all this so that Patrick can understand why we are particularly sensitive to the abduction of General Stewart.'

Charles turned back to me. 'That's the NATO background. It's secondary to our main cause for concern. That's something much nearer home.'

'Jesus!'

'Richie, you're quite sure about your telephone? We're absolutely bug-free?'

'Yes.' Since coming into the K & R business Richie had become very particular about the privacy of his communications, especially over the telephone. We had learned the hard way that a telephone handset can easily be turned into an open room microphone, that the telephone need never be picked up — need never even ring — to carry a private conversation anywhere throughout the world. Worse than that, the wire-tapper didn't even need to enter the premises. All he had to do was place a device on a telephone pole, or a wire closet or anywhere along the line inside a block of flats.

'I sweep out for bugs every day and I have an anti-wiretap system on the 'phone. Unless someone's beaming a laser mike at the window we are okay.'

Charles glanced at the curtained window as if he were reluctant to dismiss the possibility that unseen listeners had installed themselves in the building across the street.

'I mentioned that Stewart was DMO before moving to Brussels. That means he is fully conversant with the British weapon.'

'The new Trident D5?'

'No, our own secret weapon.'

'You mean, we've got one?'

It was a stupid remark, prompted by years of watching Britain run herself and her armed forces down. If I'd expected to raise a grin from Richie I was disappointed.

'Oh, yes.' Charles half-closed his eyes as if the light was hurting them. 'People tend to forget how many decisive

14

weapons were invented by the British. We were the first to develop and use tanks, we pioneered radar, jet engines, the aircraft carrier — damn it, the atom was first split at Cambridge and we did all the early work on nuclear weapons! But it is now thirty-seven years since the Bomb was dropped on Hiroshima. Science has moved a long way since then. The era of the big bang may soon be ended.'

'You're saying that nuclear weapons are out-dated?'

'Not so much out-dated as superceded. Compared with some of the things our scientists have dreamed up, the Bomb seems positively humane.'

Richie, prowling about the room, halted behind Charles and looked over his head at me.

'Charles is exaggerating, of course. What he's getting at is that you can't use nuclear weapons without everyone knowing.'

I suggested: 'Whereas you might use chemical or biological weapons?'

'Or something more sophisticated.'

Merely talking about this had made Charles tense up, though the only signs which betrayed him were the flexing of one languidly crossed leg and the tightening of his fingers on the crease of his trousers.

'What sort of weapon is it?'

I could not really expect an answer to that question, although for some reason the COBRA man had already gone far beyond the normal limits of security. He at last gave a thin smile.

'I can't tell you that. All I can say is that it is satellite-based and when it is fully developed it will completely revolutionise the whole concept of war.'

I suppose my scepticism must have shown on my face. To give me time to digest what he had said, Charles withdrew a leather cigar-case from his waistcoat pocket. He took out the third and last Montecristo, sliced it with a pocket cutter and applied a match.

'The point is,' he continued, when the end was aglow, 'that we have kept this one to ourselves. Call it an insurance policy,

15

if you like. In democratic communities governments can change their complexion overnight. Even the Atlantic Alliance could break up. So, for the moment we are not sharing BISBAS with anyone.'

'Bisbas?'

'British Independent Satellite-Based Attack System.'

Charles reached for the brandy bottle and poured a little into his glass. Richie avoided my eye. He went to twitch the curtain back a little and look down into the street.

'Where did you leave your car, Pat?'

'A couple of hundred yards away, in Parkam Street.'

'Was it Sally with you when I 'phoned?'

'Yes.'

'Did you tell her where you were going?'

'Of course not!'

'Just checking, old pal. But you did use my name, didn't you?'

'Yes,' I admitted. 'But she was half asleep. I don't suppose she noticed or cared.'

He let the curtain fall back on the darkness outside, came back to the fireside. For the first time since I'd arrived he sat down.

'Tell him why we're here, Charles.'

'We're here,' Charles said, 'because I have asked Richie to go out to Italy and find the General. I happen to be a close personal friend of Lady Stewart.'

'Then you're not here in your official capacity — from the Cabinet Office Briefing Room?'

'Yes and no,' Charles answered slowly. 'I'd rather you didn't push me on that. But Lady Stewart knows what I am doing.'

Richie was filling a pipe with the special mixture which Dunhill's made up for him — Number 753.

'I told Charles that I'd want a second opinion before I accepted,' he said. 'If you're game for it, then I am. The money is good. Very good.'

'Go out to Italy, locate Stewart and release him? Just that?'

Richie nodded, striking a match and putting it to the bowl

16

of his pipe. I was beginning to wish I had not sworn to give up smoking. The craving for a drag had come on again.

'Why not leave it to the Italians? They have their own special units, the Carabinieri's *Gruppo di Intervento Speciale* and the *Nuclei Operazioni Contro Subversione*. If they can't find him there's not much hope for a foreign group.'

'Yes, I know about the GIS and NOCS. But we're talking about a British general.' Charles spoke with startling passion, putting special emphasis on the British. 'I know he was out there in his NATO capacity but he's *our* most distinguished soldier and he holds *our* most secretive information. That's why a British group has to go out and free him. This overrides diplomatic niceties and political posturing.'

The little speech had been something of a give-away. It was a cinch that this party was being arranged without ministerial approval.

'Besides,' Charles went on in more matter-of-fact tones. 'There's so much corruption in Italian government departments — including the Ministry of the Interior. And their own police are handicapped because ordinary people are too frightened of the terrorists to inform on them. There might even be support for the kidnappers in some quarters. A NATO general is not exactly a popular hero in southern Italy.'

'Surely he was using some sort of kidnap alert system.'

'Oh, yes. All the top brass do nowadays. He had a system linked to his car. The bleeper was fitted to his wrist watch. For some reason it did not work. He may not have had time to activate it. The intelligence unit at Naples have monitors out trying to pick up a signal, but the device only has a range of five miles or so.'

I nodded. The smoke from Richie's pipe drifted past my nostrils. A fragrant mixture with plenty of Balkan leaf and Latakia. He was watching me covertly and I could tell that he desperately wanted to accept this mission.

'What about the SAS?' I said. 'Isn't this a job just up their street?'

'The SAS are ruled out.' Some exasperation was apparent

in Charles's voice. 'This will be an internal Italian problem. Their official policy is to make no concessions to terrorism. The British government will express support for that policy and confidence in the efficiency of the Italian counter-subversion agencies. It would be out of the question to use any component of our armed forces in an allied country without a request from the government concerned.'

'Don't you have your own organisations for handling things like this — MI6, or the secret intelligence service?'

Charles moved uneasily in his chair. For once his self-assurance wilted. 'Those departments have become too big, too bureaucratic. Too many people would have to know about a thing like this and that simply increases the chances of a leak. We can't afford that.'

He had not given me the real reason but I didn't press him on what must be an uncomfortable point. Newspaper revelations of Russian moles in our intelligence services were recent enough to rankle still. It was disturbing that the Cabinet Office had turned to a private agency in a crisis involving national security.

Charles read my thoughts.

'That is why my visit here is off the record. You don't know my name, we have not talked. As far as you are concerned I do not exist. Richie asked me to stay and to brief you so that you will understand the reasons behind the most difficult aspect of this assignment. As far as the record is concerned you are being retained by Lady Stewart to free her husband. My department can facilitate things for you in a number of ways while you are still in this country, not least in the matter of finance.'

I did not like the look of it. He had not mentioned the principal advantage from the British Government's point of view. If we got ourselves into any kind of trouble in Italy they would disclaim all knowledge of us.

I looked at Richie. 'You said the money was good. It would have to be before we took this one on.'

'The budget is two million sterling.' It was Charles who replied to my objection. 'Half of that relates to your fee. The

18

rest is to cover expenses and inducements for information.'

'Ransom money?'

'No. If a ransom demand is made it will be dealt with officially. But I don't think it will be. In any case by then the damage would be done.'

'Is this tax-payers' money?'

'It is not.' Charles flung me a glance of dislike. 'Funds have been made available by a private donor. He has to remain anonymous, but he's someone who stands to lose a great deal more than two million if Stewart talks.'

'You keep assuming that he will talk.'

'Yes, I am making that assumption. At first he will resist interrogation, or try to feed them mis-information. But in the end he will tell them all he knows. It will take a little time, but in the end he will tell them.'

Charles drained his brandy and stood up, still holding the cigar which he had carefully kept alight. He stooped to collect his matches from the coffee table. The hands of the little carriage clock on Richie's mantelpiece pointed to twenty-seven minutes past five.

'I think we've covered the relevant points. In fact I've gone a good deal further than I should. I want you to understand that nothing less than the nation's most vital interests are at stake here, perhaps even the balance between peace and war.'

Charles appeared to be assuming that we were going to take this job on. I got up and stood blocking his route to the hall.

'You're asking us to carry out an SAS-style operation without the resources of the SAS. Suppose we fluff it and the terrorists shoot Stewart?'

Charles was tall enough to look at me down his nose. The dislike was mutual.

'You still get your fee. You will have accomplished the main objective. If Stewart is dead he can't talk.'

TWO

Charles had departed, declining Richie's offer of breakfast. He wanted to be home before daylight. He telephoned for a radio cab and gave the number of a house on the opposite side of the Square.

'Jumpy, isn't he?' I said, when the door had closed on him. 'Does he think he's being tailed?'

'All these blokes are very sensitive nowadays. With the clamp-down on the intelligence services they never know when they may be under observation. That's why he didn't come by car. Since the Police National Computer came into use a car is like an identity label.' Instead of coming back into the sitting-room he moved towards the kitchen. 'I don't know about you but I feel like some breakfast.'

Of course we had accepted the assignment. I had seen that Richie was dead set on doing it. I was not going to be the one to stop him earning a cool million. Charles had made it clear that once we were in there could be no backing out. In fact, I had a suspicion that a point of no return had been reached very soon after my arrival at the flat. Charles had said too much to let us off the hook. If we had refused after hearing what he told us we would have become the victims of some department of dirty tricks.

I followed Richie into his kitchen-diner. The whole area was faced with pine and fitted with the latest Hauenshild cooking devices. He filled the electric kettle and plugged it in, put a pan on the hot-plate and sliced a chunk of margarine into it. He peeled six rashers of bacon off a supermarket pack and took a carton of six eggs from inside the door of the fridge.

'You could make some toast. Bread bin's over there.'

I cut four slices off the wholemeal loaf and popped the first two into the toaster.

'We'll need more than that.' Richie was tying a full-length

20

apron round himself. It was of blue and white striped material, the kind that butchers wear.

I cut two more slices, laid them beside the toaster. 'Charles took it for granted you were going to accept.'

'Charles is an old friend. I've done one or two jobs for him in the past.' He laid the rashers in a neat row in the frying pan. 'It's the time factor that worries me. We've been given a week at the outside. So we have to get out to Italy fast, start following up leads, putting out feelers, link up with the NATO signals people who are sweeping for a bleep from his tracer. We'll find him. It's surprising what you can do when you have a million to chuck around.'

The toast popped up, only half done. I pushed it down again.

'Charles told you a good deal more than he told me?'

Richie stopped prodding his rashers to look at me. 'Yes, old Pat. He did. And it's better for you not to know. You don't need to. There's always the possibility that one of us may be caught and made to talk.'

'Does Lady Stewart know that if we can't rescue him alive we're briefed to — abort him?'

'No. That's a private understanding between Charles and me.'

The toaster had begun to smoke. I pressed the release button and the slices jumped up, slightly burned. Seeing me prop them against the Moulinex coffee machine, he opened a cupboard and produced a silver toast-rack.

'Fifteen quid in the Portobello Road. The silver by itself must be worth more than that.'

'You and I aren't tackling this alone, Richie?'

'Good God, no! I telephoned a few chaps early this morning and asked them to be here between seven and eight. It's important to have Italian speakers, which narrows the field. I could not get everyone I wanted but six good chaps have said they'll come. With you and me that will make eight. I think that's the right number.'

He scooped his rashers out, slid them onto a plate and put them in the oven. He reached for the half-dozen eggs and

21

began to break them into a bowl.

'I told Charles our fee would have to be a million at least. Two hundred thousand goes to the firm. That allows me to hand a hundred grand to each member of my squad. Equal shares, of course.'

He put butter into a saucepan and began to beat the eggs energetically with a whisk. He was one of those people who could go without a night's sleep and show no after-effects. Any project which offered the spice of danger and fast action stimulated him. The brief given him by Charles was tailor-made.

'We shall need two cars, Pat. That's going to be your department. Fast cars with load-carrying and cross-country capability. I leave it to you what you get and where you get them.'

'If speed is a factor wouldn't it be quicker to fly out to Italy and get cars there?'

'Not much. By road we can be in Rome quite early tomorrow morning. We need cars to carry our equipment. It's not the sort of stuff you can take on an aircraft. Don't worry about expense. Where this operation is concerned the sky's the limit.'

While Charles had been talking to me, Richie, prowling about his sitting-room, had been working his plans out in his mind. Knowing him I could be sure that safety and prudence would be the last considerations.

'Charles said we would have support for as long as we were in this country. What exactly did he mean by that?'

'I'll tell you my plans when everyone is here. No point in going over it twice. How's the time?'

'Just coming up to half-past five.'

'Be a good chap and lay the table, will you? Put out for three. I asked Tro to come early.'

'Tro?'

'Tro Mantorin. Cutlery's in that drawer, cups and plates in the cupboard above.'

He tipped the frothing eggs into a saucepan and frowned in concentration as he adjusted the heat of the hot-plate. He was not usually as cagey as this. I assumed it was because he knew that he had abruptly escalated the operations of his new venture, committed himself to something far more risky than he had ever contemplated when he set the business up.

I'd just found the wooden pepper and salt mills and put them on the table when the entry-phone extension in the kitchen buzzed. Richie answered it briefly and then returned to his eggs.

'That's Tro. Can you answer the door? I don't want to burn these scrambled eggs.'

Tro made good time from the street entrance up to the flat. In less than a minute the bell rang. I went to open the door.

My look of surprise was a bad start.

'Are you Tro?'

The young woman standing on the landing stared back at me, frowning. Late twenties, I guessed. Might have been attractive if she'd bothered about her appearance.

'Who are you?'

'I'm Patrick. Patrick Malone.'

'How long are you going to just stand there? Do you mind if I come in?'

I stood back quickly, holding the door open for her. She swept past me, unslinging the cylindrical bag she carried on a strap over one shoulder. The details of her figure were obscured by a leather jerkin with Mexican style stitching. It was sleeveless, exposing arms covered by a blue sweater with elbow patches. Clean but faded jeans hugged her legs. She was wearing garish red and blue sneakers. Two small silk scarves, one blue and one white, were knotted round her neck.

'Let me take that for you.'

I put a hand out for her bag. She quickly switched it to the other side, beyond my reach. My misguided chivalry was not appreciated.

She tramped to the far end of the hall, dumped the bag and took off the jerkin. As she reached up to hang it on the stand a segment of sun-tanned flesh showed between the waistband of her jeans and the bottom of her sweater. She had a slim, athletic figure. Diet or hard exercise had flattened her curves.

23

'Tro,' Richie called from the kitchen. 'Come on in.'

She ignored me and went through to the kitchen. I had the impression that she knew the flat already. She was not Richie's usual type. He specialised in sophisticated London socialites, but his tastes were catholic. He might have wanted this one for variety, like grits in a balanced diet.

I followed in my own time. Richie's reception of Tro had been perfunctory. He was taking his eggs off the hot-plate.

'Patrick, can you butter three slices of toast? These eggs are ready. Have a good run down, Tro?'

'It was okay. But I was caught doing well over the ton by an unmarked police car. Bloody unfair!'

'Did they book you? You can lose your licence for that nowadays.'

'I think it will be okay. One of the cops recognised my name. He happened to be a racing fan.'

'Tro made it into Formula One before she switched to rallying,' Richie explained. 'You must have heard of her.'

The penny dropped. *That* Tro. She had looked very different wearing a Griffin crash helmet. Her real name was Katrina Mantorin. She was the girl who had carved her way through Formula Three and Formula Two and seemed set for a career in Grand Prix motor-racing. But something had gone wrong. Perhaps she really was not tough enough for the top league. Perhaps that predominantly male elite had resented the intrusion of a female. The Press had not helped, referring to her in all their reports as "the lady". They had made the most of a couple of spectacular crashes which had written off some expensive machinery. Whatever the reason, Ms Mantorin had abruptly given up racing and switched to the less chauvinistic world of rallying. She had quickly adapted herself and was soon competing with the best in the World Rally Championship. If I remembered rightly her relaxations were water-skiing, hang-gliding and sky-diving.

'Yes, I have. You certainly showed the lads a clean pair of heels in the Rally of the Forests.'

'Thanks.' She said it dismissively. Gradually I was to realise that it was a mistake to make any remark which implied surprise at a woman performing as well as men.

Richie knew the form. He treated her with off-hand casualness. She responded by some thawing of her aggressively defensive manner. She watched us putting the breakfast things onto the table. It gave her a kick to see men doing chores that were usually left to women.

I managed to take a couple of sly peeks at her without catching her eye; she might have made the mistake of thinking that I was ogling her. The face was oval, with high cheek bones. She had a well-defined nose and a rather small mouth. Two little ridges gave her upper lip a slightly pouting expression. Her russety-brown hair had been carelessly hauled back and fastened in a knot on the top of her head. It gave her a cheeky look which I was sure was not intended. She wore no make-up, and might very well not have washed her face on getting up. The long dark eyelashes were an incongruously feminine feature.

Richie drew the curtains back before we sat down round the table. Over the roofs of London the sky had already lightened. Traffic was beginning to flow in the street below.

'I appreciate the invitation to breakfast,' Tro said. She plastered butter thick onto her toast. That slim build was not due to dieting. 'But why so early?'

'Tro, you remember that argument we had about women being excluded from the Marines and the SAS and outfits like that?'

'Yes.' She nodded vigorously, talking through munched bread. 'Menial jobs like secretaries and cooks and drivers. The Baader-Meinhof were the first to realise that we can be just as tough as men.'

I was pouring out the coffee, making sure to fill her cup *last*.

'Well,' Richie said. 'I'm going to give you your chance.'

She was very smart. She swallowed hurriedly and looked at him hard.

'It's something to do with this General who's been kidnapped?'

'That's an inspired guess. If I didn't know you better I'd

25

put it down to feminine intuition.'

'Bollocks! It makes sense. You want me because I'm bilingual in Italian.'

'And you can drive a car.'

'Oh, Christ! Not the bloody chauffeur bit. I might have guessed. How do you come into it?'

'We've been asked to spring him.'

'Jesus!' She looked at me, for the first time considering me as a viable human organism. 'The three of us?'

'I've another five chaps coming. I wanted you here first. It's a tough assignment. They'll be more likely to accept if I can tell them that you've already come in on it. You will, won't you?'

Tro's face expressed disgust. 'The old machismo again. It's pathetic.'

She crammed egg, bacon and a bite of toast into her mouth, chewed hard and then started talking through the mush.

'I heard a news flash on the car radio. *Colonna Nuova* claim they've got him. They're much better organised than the old Red Brigades. You've really got a problem, but I suppose you realise that. What do you intend to do?'

'Briefly, we're going to take two cars and some gear out to Italy and try to find him. When we do we go in and get him out. Our cover is that we're a rally car and service vehicle. You and Patrick would be the drivers and the rest of us the wrenches.'

Her eyes rested appraisingly on my face again, then moved to my hands. I concealed the fact that this was the first I had heard of Richie's bright idea.

'Does he drive?'

'Patrick specialises in security driving. He can make a car do what he wants.'

She nodded, suspending judgement on that point. The next question was predictable.

'What's the car?'

'Don't know yet. Patrick will be onto that as soon as people are up and about. The point is, are you on?'

Tro had demolished her bacon and eggs, leaving Richie and

me far behind. She put her knife and fork down and grabbed the marmalade.

'Yes, of course. I should have thought that was obvious.'

After breakfast, just to make a point, Tro left us two men to clear the table and do the washing up. She paid a lengthy visit to the bathroom.

'She's quite a girl, isn't she?' Richie said, leaning over the sink. 'Don't try tangling with her. She'll break your arm and throw you over one shoulder.'

'You said chaps,' I reminded him. 'Six good chaps.'

'Well, she *is* a chap really, isn't she? Besides, terrorism is unisex these days.'

'Any more of your chaps female?'

'No. Just Tro. I reckoned one like her would be enough.'

The Saab Turbo I was using was a spin-off from Richie's quality car business. I had picked it up in Tunisia when I had gone out there to collect a Phantom II Rolls-Royce he was buying. It had the unusual quality of being bullet-proofed, a fact which was not apparent on casual inspection. Richie and I had proved its indestructibility the hard way. He'd had the damage made good and the bullet marks cosmetically repaired. When the Rolls's and Bentleys were sold he decided to keep the Saab for his new business venture. As it was the old Combi type with a hatchback opening into a capacious load platform it would do very well as the service car of our mock-up rally team.

Bill Garland was an old friend from my rallying days. He had brought his Audi Quattro into second place in the recent Rally of the Forests. He would have won if he hadn't rolled it in the final stage and allowed Katrina Mantorin to pip him. The Quattro was turbo-charged and had four-wheel drive. Its speed and cross-country capability were just what we needed. In its rally livery it would make our cover story more credible, especially going through the French and Italian Customs.

The question was, could Bill be persuaded to part with it?

Bill's team headquarters was at Isleworth. He was always there by eight o'clock, the time his mechanics were expected to turn up. I picked up a taxi in the King's Road and arrived at ten past eight. He had rented a small warehouse which he had equipped as a garage with lathes, hoists, power tools, rolling road — everything needed to prepare a car for modern rallying. A section at the back had been partitioned off to provide an office and a rest-room for the mechanics.

When I arrived the "wrenches" were still climbing into their overalls. Bill was at his desk checking through the morning mail. The Quattro, fresh from its triumph in the Rally of the Forests, was on jacks. Its wheels were off and its engine was on a stand near the work-bench. The body was painted in a brilliant scheme of red, white and blue, the colours of Bill's sponsors. It was covered with advertising decals. The only evidence of his roll were a few dents and scratches. They added to its authentic appearance.

Beside it stood a brand-new grey Audi Quattro, fresh from Barclay European.

Bill was a cheerful, bouncy little man with curly hair and twinkling eyes. At first he just laughed when I said I wanted to buy his rally car, tried to sell me the new Quattro instead — at a considerable profit. He became serious when I told him I'd pay any reasonable price he cared to name. He was a businessman as well as an ace rally driver. To help him make up his mind I named a figure.

'Would sixty grand persuade you?'

He blinked rapidly but otherwise his expression did not change. The new Audi had cost him eighteen thousand, so that left him thirty-two for development expenses.

'Make it seventy and we're in business.'

'I can make it seventy if you'll include a full set of spares.'

'Okay. You'll want tyres too?'

'A couple of spares will do.'

'You're not going rallying, then?'

'No.'

Bill put down the pen he had been doodling with. His curiosity was obvious.

'I heard you were with Richie Bryer in this new outfit he's got going.'

'That's right.'

'What are you up to, then?'

'If I was prepared to answer that I wouldn't be paying you over twice the value of the car.'

'Point taken. When do you want to collect her?'

'Trouble is, Bill, I've got to be on my way within an hour. Can you put it together in that time?'

'No problem. My lads are used to working fast and they've already done the engine. What about axle-ratios and so on? Do you want maximum speed or performance low down?'

We discussed gear ratios and tyre patterns for a few minutes, then Bill went out to give instructions to his mechanics. I could see that his agile brain was already working out how he could make use of this unexpected windfall.

The mechanics went to work with the methodical urgency which enabled them to change a gearbox in twenty minutes on a wind-swept mountain road.

I used Bill's telephone to call my own flat. It rang for a long time before Sally answered. I told her that I would not be back, she'd have to get her own breakfast and let herself out of the flat.

'I'm sorry about this, Sally,' I finished. 'I'll see you when I get back.'

'Not if I see you first.'

At half-past nine I drove the Audi out through the doors of the warehouse, leaving Bill with the promise that he'd have the money later that day — in cash.

In its brilliant and variegated paintwork the rally car stood out conspicuously among the monochromatic saloons of the commuters driving into town. I had a slow run back to Melton Square, with no chance to sample its performance. I parked as close to the Saab as I could and walked to the flat.

Richie was in the sitting-room talking to a couple of strangers, with Tro listening in.

'Okay, Patrick? You got the car all right?'

'Yes. I promised we'd get seventy grand out to Bill some time today.'

Richie nodded and waved a hand towards the two newcomers.

'Patrick, this is Clement — and Frank.'

Richie made the introductions without bothering about surnames. The man he had introduced as Clement was staring at me steadily with remote grey eyes. Though he was still a young man — around thirty, perhaps — there was a world of experience in those eyes. You somehow knew that they had learned to look on mayhem and remain detached. He was lanky and wiry, with a hawkish nose and a straight, thin mouth. His dress was casual. Shirt, cardigan and corduroy trousers were all fawn. No tie. His crossed feet were in a pair of suede ankle-boots.

He nodded to me from his chair, making no attempt to rise. A deepening of the two creases in his cheeks might have been interpreted as a smile.

'Clement's come down from Yorkshire. He was in the SAS for a spell before he came out of the Army.'

That meant he was super-fit, trained in the martial arts, a crack shot, familiar with every modern hand-gun, rifle, or machine-gun, an expert on explosives, forcible entry, scaling and mountaineering and God knows what other diabolical skills. If he was a recent product he was probably conversant with the latest high technology. It crossed my mind that Clement might still be in the Army, as well as a member of the SAS. Perhaps this was one of the ways in which Charles was giving us practical help.

'Frank's real name is Franco, but we call him Frank when he's in England. He's married to an English girl — very attractive, too.'

Franco stood up to shake my hand warmly, continental fashion. He was a complete contrast to Clement. His appearance was unmistakably Latin with rather fleshy cheeks, white teeth, naturally dark skin and a burgeoning of stubble shadowing his chin. His hair was dark and curly. His eyes beamed from behind large, horn-rimmed spectacles. He was on the short side, but his hands were large and his grip strong.

30

'Glad to meet you, Patrick.'

His English was perfect, with a faint American flavour.

'Frank runs a nice little business importing Italian wines,' Richie said with a grin. 'He has excellent contacts in Italy, haven't you, Frank?'

To judge by Franco's answering smile, accompanied by a very Latin shrug, those contacts were the kind that enabled him to by-pass the *Guardia di Finanza* and HM Customs and Excise. He gave Tro a nervous glance. She averted her face. There was tension between these two. Frank had probably switched on the Mediterranean charm for her benefit and been rewarded with a flea in his ear.

'Did you get the Audi?' she asked now.

'Yes.'

She stood up. 'Let's take a run in it.'

'You haven't time,' Ritchie said. 'The others should be here any minute.'

'Well, we'll just have a look at it. Come on, Patrick.'

'Five minutes, no more.'

Tro pretended not to hear. As we left the flat I noted that though she did not want you to stand aside for her she liked to be first through doors. Following her I was amused by her rapid, slightly hen-toed walk. Any suggestion of wiggle was ruthlessly suppressed.

When we emerged from the lift we found a couple of men waiting to go up. I was certain that they were two more of Richie's chaps, though we didn't exchange words. They stood back politely to let us emerge before they moved into the lift. Neither of them missed a single detail of our appearance.

Tro ran an expert, appraising eye over the Audi Quattro's aerodynamic, wedge-shaped body, with its spoilers front and rear. She stooped to inspect the wide-section tyres and the all-independent suspension system. She opened the door and slipped behind the steering wheel in the left-hand drive seat. Something about her changed as she settled herself. It was as if she had come back into her own element. She adjusted the seat, tapped the pedals with her feet, checked all round visibility and flicked her eyes over the essential instruments grouped within the upper arc of the steering wheel.

She pressed a button to lower the window. I had to stoop to talk to her.

'Brake horse power?'

'About two hundred DIN in standard form. Bill reckons about two seventy on this one.'

'Five cylinders, right?'

'Five cylinders, fuel injection, turbo-charged. You have five speeds, of course. Power steering too but it's not obtrusive.'

She nodded, reserving judgement. She started the engine, listened to its throaty roar with her head half turned. Her expression had softened, almost to tenderness.

'I've never used four-wheel drive. What's it feel like?'

'Haven't had a chance to test it out, but she seems to grab the road like a leech.'

'Don't forget this is the car that won the Lombard RAC rally — first and second places.'

When we got back to the flat the two we had met outside the lift were consuming a continental breakfast. Johnnie Wilson was a squat, almost corpulent fellow with a ready grin and crinkly black hair. He came from Liverpool and had ridden down on his six-cylinder Kawasaki. His voice was rich and fruity with the suggestion of a chuckle or laugh not far below the surface. Like Richie he had been a mercenary in the days when freelance soldiering was a respectable occupation.

The other man at the table had a face so pale that it seemed to have been dusted with white chalk. The features were etched on it as starkly as if they had been drawn with charcoal. His name was Nick. I didn't catch the surname when Richie introduced him. It sounded like Cantariu. He obviously had Central European blood in him, but had lived for some years in Israel. Now he was an instructor at an Outward Bound school in Wales. Like the others he had a good knowledge of Italian.

'Bring your coffee into the sitting-room,' Richie told them. 'We can't wait any longer for Stan.'

The little travelling clock was announcing ten o'clock with its Lilliputian bell when a strong fist hammered the knocker of the front door.

Stan was a huge man, as tall as Clement and as broad as Johnnie. I put his weight at over twenty stone. He was fair-haired and red-faced with the ambling gait of a good-natured bear. He had been a member of PATU, the Rhodesian Police's anti-terrorist unit under Ian Smith, and had not fancied staying on when Mr Mugabe came to power. He'd had to leave all his savings behind and was not entitled to any Social Security benefits in the UK. He was working as a Bristol furniture remover's heavy man and thankful to have a job. Richie had met him in the seventies when he was operating a sanction-beating run from Zaïre. Stan was the only member of the group who had no Italian.

Richie now gave his complete squad five minutes to get acquainted, though acquainted was hardly the right word. They were a variegated bunch but had one thing in common. Each of them gave an impression of almost unnatural alertness and wariness. You felt they had tremendous energy under strict control, a characteristic of racing drivers, sky divers, high climbers and others who are drawn to activities which put life at risk.

They were still guarded in their attitude to each other, and certainly not mixing like guests at a drinks party. Richie had only told them that he wanted them for a "rough old job".

When he persuaded them to come through from the kitchen-diner to the sitting-room they did so reluctantly. They were too restless to commit themselves to the chairs or sofa. Only Franco and I sat down. Johnnie and Nick went to the French window that opened onto the balcony. Stan perched on the arm of the sofa, Tro propped her behind on the edge of the table, Clement leaned against the door-jamb. From there he could see through the hall to the front door.

They were not a captive audience. Richie knew they would not be receptive to a long harangue. Very quickly he named each person there and gave a brief sketch of their background. Half a dozen pairs of shrewd eyes flicked covertly from face to face. They rested a little longer on Tro when her name came up. She managed to look suitably layed back.

'Before I put you in the picture I must know whether you are in this with me or not. It's going to be tough and dangerous and you know me well enough to realise that I don't use those words lightly. You'll have heard that General Stewart has been kidnapped in Italy, probably by a new wing of the Red Brigades called *Colonna Nuova*. We are going out there to find him and release him. We'll be up against an organisation that has a record of murder and violence. We will have no official approval or backing either from the British or Italian Governments. But the pay-off is good. Eight hundred thousand to split between us. Equal shares, of course.'

'One hundred and fourteen thousand, three hundred each — approximately,' Franco said at once. 'Pounds sterling, of course?'

'Of course. But you've got your sums wrong. There's eight of us — if you all come in.'

Franco's spectacles reflected light as he shot a surprised look in the direction of Tro. She stared back at him expressionlessly.

'Where is it payable?' Johnnie asked.

'Anywhere you like. Zurich, Brussels, Monaco — you name it. Now, do I count you all in?'

'Of course,' Tro said, angered by Franco's assumption that she was only there for decoration. 'Isn't that what we're here for?'

It had the effect Richie had been counting on. If a woman had accepted these men were not going to refuse.

'No abstentions. All right then . . .'

Richie's briefing was terse and to the point. He did not tell them more than he had to. Speed was of the essence. They had to reach their target within a week at the outside. The means of transport would be cars. Their cover for the purpose of getting through Customs and into Italy would be that they were a rally crew going out to compete in the Appenine Rally. Once there they'd set about picking up a lead to the whereabouts of the General, offering rewards for information which would be hard to resist. He did not mention Charles, nor Lady Stewart.

'The stakes are very high,' he finished. 'In fact they could hardly be higher. So we stop at nothing to bring this off.'

'These funds you mention,' said Johnnie, the mercenary, from his window. 'Have they already been made available? I mean, do we get an advance?'

'I'm flying to Geneva this afternoon to make sure of that very point. You'll pick me up on your way out. By that time the financial side will be tied up. Meantime, I'll issue you with expense money from my own supply.'

'The reward is not very generous,' Johnnie persisted. 'Johnny Miller got a quarter of a million for playing four days' golf at Bophutatswana.'

'Then I suggest you take up golf,' Tro snapped.

'You said we stop at nothing.' Stan reached forward to put his coffee cup down on the table. 'There could be killings. Have we any immunity from prosecution by the Italians?'

'We have no immunity. Anything we do is on our own heads. Open that door, will you, Nick?' Richie nodded towards the French window. 'It's getting very stuffy in here.'

Nick turned the handle and pushed open one half of the door to the balcony. A shaft of oblique sunlight slanted through it across the carpet.

'The deterrent these sort of people usually rely on,' Clement said quietly from the doorway, 'is the threat to kill their captive if they are cornered.'

'That's a risk we have to take.'

Clement nodded seriously. He had got the message. Stewart was expendable. The principal objective was to get to him before he talked.

It was coming up to half-past ten. Richie went to switch on the radio for the news bulletin. The first item was the emergency meeting of the North Atlantic Council which had been convened at Brussels. The NATO Situations Centre was on a red alert basis. The Military Committee wanted Member States to agree on a uniform policy in the event of a Soviet invasion of Poland. As usual, the politically motivated Ministers of the fifteen nations involved had adopted conflicting attitudes.

35

The abduction of Stewart had been relegated to second place. That morning in Rome, where time was an hour ahead of London, a telephone call to the *Corriera della Sera* offices had led the authorities to the first communiqué from the kidnappers. It had been found in a dustbin near the Quirinale, and was accompanied by the General's signet ring. The statement, issued by *Colonna Nuova*, stated simply that General Stewart had been arrested as a tool of NATO imperialism. He was being held in a people's prison, where he would be interrogated and tried by qualified lawyers. No terms for his release had so far been proposed.

'A people's prison,' Stan said. 'What the hell does that mean?'

'A tiny room or cellar in some safe house. Probably furnished with a bed and nothing else. He may be very restricted. Corrado Santini was kept bound, gagged and blindfolded for fifty days with plugs in his ears. Or he might be in a small tent to prevent him seeing his surroundings or captors. He's probably in some town or city. They usually take their captives to places where car movements and strange faces don't excite curiosity.'

Richie always kept a supply of British and foreign currency in his safe in case he had to go off on a job at a time when the banks were closed. He opened it now and issued us each with some spending money. I was given a couple of hundred in French francs for the run across France, just in case the half-dozen credit cards I carried were not acceptable.

'Franco, I want you to take the first available 'plane to Rome. Rustle up your contacts and find out as much as you can about police measures so far. They may have some leads. If not, go to the underworld. We should be in Rome by nine or ten tomorrow morning.'

'You'll contact me at my flat?' Franco readjusted his spectacles and got to his feet, anxious to waste no time.

'Palazzo Mellini, yes. Clem, will you keep in touch with that Ordnance Corps Major we spoke to? Fix up a rendezvous where we can pick up the stuff when they've got it ready.'

Clement nodded and moved aside to let Franco pass.

'Johnnie, I think we can use CB radios for our own communications. Would you handle that? We need a couple of car sets and say half a dozen hand-held sets.'

'What'll I use for cash? What you've given me won't cover it.'

'I'll give you another grand. Okay?'

Johnnie nodded, his chubby face creasing into a smile.

'Stan, will you contact the ferry services at Dover about hovercraft services this afternoon? We'll want them to put our cars on the first available service after we arrive. And ring the touring services of the RAC at Croydon for the latest information on road and motorway conditions through to Rome. We'll need maps of Italy, too. Sandfords in Long Acre is the best place. Get the largest scale you can. Taxi would be the quickest way. Tro, would you contact the London correspondent of the *Corriere della Sera*? He has an office in one of the *Daily Telegraph* buildings. It's in the 'phone book. Get the latest gen on the kidnapping. The wire services may know more than we've heard on the radio. Nick, we're going to need —'

'I'm sorry, Richie. You'll have to count me out.'

'*What*?'

Richie was unable to keep the wrath out of his voice. I saw Clement's pallid eyes swing towards Nick. The latter's chalky face had gone even paler.

'I'm wanted in Italy on a murder charge. If they still had the death sentence I'd chance it, but I could not take a life sentence in one of their prisons.'

Richie took a moment to control his anger. During the short silence everyone was staring at Nick. The tufts of black hair on his cheekbones stuck out as straight as a porcupine's quills.

'I wish you'd said that before, Nick.'

'I assumed we would have some immunity from arrest, but if people are liable to be killed and —'

'It does not matter,' Richie cut in on him. 'In fact, it may be all for the best. We can use you without you having to go out there. It would be useful to have a contact here. You'd stay in the flat and hold the fort. Of course, you'll still get your share of the loot.'

Richie had been thinking very quickly. That promise of the reward had betrayed his concern about Nick. The prospect of a hundred thousand pounds was an incentive for him to be a good boy and keep his mouth shut. But with Johnnie's and Clement's eyes still fixed on him Nick knew that he must now be regarded as a security risk. To them he was a stranger. I could guess how their minds were working. They were not going to like setting off on a mission which would be blown if Nick had decided that there was more to be made out of informing on them than joining in.

The telephone ringing on Richie's desk broke the tense hush. He crossed the room quickly.

'Hello? Yes.' He listened for a moment. 'That's out of the question! I haven't time. We're on a very tight count-down as it is . . .Well, that would help but we can't be with her for long . . . Okay, we'll look out for them.'

He put the 'phone down and turned to Nick.

'Nick, I want you to stay in the flat and take any messages. I want this 'phone permanently manned. Is that understood?'

Nick nodded, very nervous. He understood all too well. Richie had said: We stop at nothing. Nick was no longer a member of the action group. He knew that he had *better* stay in the flat.

'Come on, Patrick.' Richie was heading for the hall.

'Where are we going?'

'Into town. I'll explain in the lift.'

The small lift — "capacity limited to four persons" — sank earthwards. Richie said: 'That was Charles on the 'phone. Lady Stewart is in London, Brown's Hotel. She flew in this morning. He wants us to see her. I could hardly refuse when he said he'd lay on a police car. And we can use it as a taxi for another call I want to make in Mayfair.'

Charles must have had a lot of pull with the Metropolitan Police to bring a police car to our door so promptly. The Rover 3.5 SE was double parked bang opposite the entrance, its engine still running. The two constables sitting in the front

38

seats glanced at us with curiosity but asked no questions.

Richie and I climbed into the back seat and the car leaped forward. The blue lights were flashing and the siren hollering as we moved out of Melton Square, turning towards the Fulham Road. Our driver was good, probably Class A from the Police Driving School at Hendon. He carved a way through the morning traffic like a hot knife through butter, blasting private cars out of his way, passing on the wrong side of islands, crashing traffic lights whey they were red. Charles must have given us an Emergency priority. We raced along the King's Road at between sixty and seventy, rocking in our seats as we swerved round cars, buses, lorries. The professional drivers, hearing us coming, pulled aside to make way for us. Once we had to brake viciously as a Senior Citizen asserted her rights on a zebra crossing.

'Did you know Lady Stewart writes under the name of Diana Hunter?' Richie asked me as we sat back in our seats again.

'Diana Hunter the novelist?'

I'd read some of her books. Very meaty stuff with more than a touch of the occult creeping in. One of them had been adapted for television serialisation recently and had aroused conflicting, almost passionate opinions.

'She's a remarkable woman.' Richie's phrase reminded me that Charles had said the same thing about her husband. 'They were married in 1953. She had a son in 1955. He's in the army now. Army Air Corps. There was a second child in 1957, a girl, but she died when she was only a few weeks old. That was when she took up writing. I guess it was a kind of escape. Hunter was her maiden name.'

'You've met her?'

'No.'

His information must have come from Charles. We were slowing momentarily for Sloane Square. It was crammed with mid-morning traffic. Our driver blasted a way through, not hesitating to the use the pavement to get round the back of a Harrods delivery van. The insistent hee-hawing of the siren echoed off the tall buildings surrounding the square. Once through we built up speed again, using the authority of the flashing lights to crash two sets of traffic lights that were showing red.

'Have you known Nick for long?'

'About a year.' Richie was staring ahead, unable to take his eyes off the road. We swung right, cutting through Belgrave Square, and plunged into the maelstrom of vehicles at Hyde Park Corner. 'He did a very clean job for me in Algeria. You see, Pat, I didn't have much time to drum up a squad for this job, especially as I wanted to have Italian-speakers.'

'Can Nick keep his mouth shut? A lot is going to depend on that.'

'It'll be all right. Don't you worry.'

The slowest part of the journey was the quarter mile along Piccadilly before the turning into Albermarle Street. Traffic was nose to tail, but the drivers of buses and taxis edged aside to enable the clamouring police car to cork-screw a tortuous way through the jam. Just seven minutes after leaving Melton Square our driver stopped outside the discreet entrance to Brown's Hotel.

'We'll wait for you here, sir,' his mate said. The deference implicit in the "sir" did not extend to opening the door for us.

Inside the hotel all was courtesy, elegance and calm. A manager in tails with a rose in his buttonhole informed us that the Lady Stewart was in the Victoria Suite on the second floor. After ringing through to her he summoned a porter to take us up in the lift.

The General's wife received us in the hall of her suite as courteously as if we had been weekend guests at her Brussels home. She must have been in her late fifties but she had a dignity and presence that would turn heads as effectively as a fashion model. She stood tall and very erect. Her mouth was firm and her gaze steady. Of course, she had not slept and there were deep shadows under her eyes. But she had herself absolutely under control. Though she had tints of grey in her hair there was still a feminine attractiveness about her. Even in the crisis she had dressed with care. She had used make-up to mask the signs of fatigue and stress.

'Do come in.' A pleasant voice, educated but unsnobbish.

We followed her into an elegant sitting-room, furnished with genuine antiques. There had been no shaking of hands.

'It was good of you to come,' she said when she had got us seated. She herself was sitting very upright on a high-backed wing-chair. 'Charles explained to me that you have very little time, so I won't offer you anything. He told me that you had agreed to his proposal. I am very grateful.'

'I'm not sure how much you know, Lady Stewart.' I sensed that Richie was uneasy in her presence and I could understand why. 'Was there something you wanted to ask me? Charles was very insistent on my coming to see you.'

'Yes. I told him that I can help you.'

'I beg your — '

'I can help you to find him.'

'How — uh — how's that?'

She crossed her hands on her lap. They were beautifully shaped, with long, sensitive fingers.

'Dick and I are very close.' She forced a smile to her lips. 'That's not surprising as we have been married for thirty-six years. But ours is not an ordinary closeness. I will not try to explain it but we maintain a kind of contact, even when we are apart. I don't mean actual messages of the verbal sort. It's simply that I am aware of whether he is well or ill. I feel it when anything violent or exciting happens to him. I knew at five past six yesterday that he was under duress.'

She was regarding Richie with her serene hazel eyes. He could not look away.

'Didn't they inform you through NATO channels?' Richie challenged her. 'I thought their satellite communications system was very hot.'

'I was at the house of a friend, so they could not reach me.'

Richie was contemplating her thoughtfully. I could read his mind. We had come barrelling through the London traffic to listen to a woman whose mind was deranged by shock and grief telling us that she had supernatural powers. I gave him credit for pretending to take her seriously.

'Can you tell us any more? Like, where he is now and what

his condition is?'

'He is conscious but in distress. It may be pain and it may be fear but the distress is acute. I cannot tell you where he is except that I think it is dark. Perhaps I will know more when I get to Italy.'

'You are going out to Italy?'

'Even if I do not achieve anything I will at least be nearer to Dick. I am sure that he will know that I am not far — not far away.'

Her control wavered for a moment.

'The Embassy are making arrangements. If you contact them they'll tell you where to find me. We must keep in touch. We can help each other.'

Richie cleared his throat. 'Lady Stewart, I hate to ask you this, but — how do you think your husband will react to their — ' he paused before adding, 'methods of interrogation.'

'You mean torture. Dick knew very well that this might happen to him. We once talked about it. He is a man of great courage. You know that he won the VC, as well as the MC and a DSO with Bar. He was mentioned five times in despatches. But he had one great fear — that he would break under torture.'

Her eyes had gone unnaturally bright, shining with moisture which she would not allow to congeal into tears.

'We — must not allow that to happen, must we?' She put a hand up and clenched it. 'It is unthinkable that a glorious career should end in an abject capitulation.'

'You think he could be broken?'

'Anyone can be broken — if the right methods are used. You see, Dick has an Achilles heel — '

She wanted to go on speaking, but she could not. She pressed her lips tightly together. Her throat moved as she swallowed, trying to recover her voice.

'You see, he did a mission behind the German lines during the war in Italy. He was captured in civilian dress so he became a prisoner of the Gestapo. He was kept for six weeks in a cell not much bigger than a coffin — in total darkness. That is why you have to find him quickly. You understand?'

42

In that moment I had a flash of extra-sensory perception myself. I was certain she knew that our brief was to abort him if we could not rescue him.

'I want my husband back, Mr Bryer. I know that the British Government has to pretend that they have absolute confidence in the Italians, but I do not. My family have not the means to offer a big enough ransom, so I intend to see what I can do by a personal appeal.'

Richie caught my eye and stood up.

'I will be in Rome tomorrow morning. I will make contact with the Embassy so that we shall know as soon as you arrive. But you must appreciate that we are working under cover. It would be fatal if any word of this mission leaked out.'

She rose from the chair, still gazing intently at Richie.

'I understand. You will bring him back for me, won't you?'

The police car was still waiting, parked nonchalantly on a double yellow line. The driver started his engine as he saw us coming.

'Can you take us to South Audley Street before we go back to Chelsea?'

'Just let me check my control, sir.'

The co-driver picked up his mike, exchanged a few words on Tango Three O's frequency. He turned back to Richie.

'That's all right, sir. We're cleared to take you anywhere you want. Round the Square, Fred,' he told the driver, 'and along Mount Street.'

This time the driver did not need to use the blue lights and siren for the short drive to South Audley Street.

'We've got to do what she asks,' I said, as we swung round the corner at the top of the Square.

'Who?'

'Lady Stewart.'

'We're going to try.'

'I mean bring him back alive — despite what Charles said.'

'Yes, old pal. That's our primary aim.'

Richie half turned towards me. I could only see his glass eye. It was as dead as a polished topaz.

At his directions the police car turned right into South Audley Street and parked opposite the small shop at Number 62. The sign above it read: *Communications Control Systems Ltd.* It was demurely tucked between a gentlemen's tailoring establishment and an oriental carpet emporium.

Richie walked across the pavement and disappeared through the door. The window and front shop were filled with interesting but harmless toys. I glimpsed a variety of cordless telephones, infra-red detector scopes, personal defence devices as well as a bomb blanket and a range of bullet-resistant vests.

Richie was in the shop for ten minutes. When he emerged he was accompanied by two assistants carrying four sizeable cardboard cartons. The policemen made room for them among the cones, lamps and warning signs they carried in the boot.

We went home by way of Cadogan Place, where Richie rushed into a branch of Coutts & Co, his bankers. He came out with his A5-sized leather money-wallet bulging.

We were back at Melton Square by 11.42, again thanks to the blue lights and siren. The dash into Mayfair had occupied just over an hour. Without the assistance of the police car it would have taken us twice the time. The driver had enjoyed himself. The two cops were quite disappointed that we didn't want them any more, but Richie felt that we'd attract too much attention to ourselves if we went everywhere to an accompaniment of sirens and flashing lights.

Stan had not returned from his trip to Long Acre. Johnnie, very pleased with himself, had purchased two Cobra 21X FM sets for the cars and half a dozen hand-held Harvard sets for external use.

'How long will it take to fit sets in the cars, Johnnie?'

'Five minutes. I've done the Audi already. All I have to do is slap a magnetic aerial on the roof and SWR it to the set.'

'Could you do the Saab now? I'd like it in before we leave for the airport. There are some cartons in the boot. Mind how you handle them.'

'ROAC came through,' Clement said, as Johnnie went out with a box under his arm. 'Made a rendezvous for us to pick the stuff up at the MVEE testing track at 1230 hours.'

Richie looked at his watch. 'We'll just have time for that on the way to the airport, but we'll have to move. Any other messages, Nick?'

Nick had kept silent and detached from the group. It emphasised how far out on a limb he was. Now, pleased to be of use and eager to help, he came forward with a pad in his hand.

'You had seven calls. I made a note of them all and took their numbers in case you wanted to ring back.'

'Thanks.' Richie ran his eye down the list. He went into the sitting-room to do some telephoning and closed the door.

'Get anything from the *Corriere*?' I asked Tro. I'd been unable to get Lady Stewart off my mind, and the old soldier who had a phobia about confined spaces.

'No more communiqués from *Colonna Nuova*,' she told me. 'The security forces — you know, NOCS and the GIS — have raided masses of houses. There's a rumour that *Colonna Nuova* are demanding the release of all their *brigadisti* pals serving prison sentences. Did Clem say you're going out to the MVEE circuit?'

'Yes.'

'Why don't I come with you in the Audi? I mean it would be a marvellous place to try it out.'

So it was a convoy of two vehicles that set out ten minutes later. Johnnie stayed in the flat with Nick, waiting for Stan to return. Clement and I rode in the Saab. Richie went with Tro in the Audi.

That gave us a chance to try out the CB equipment Johnnie had installed. With the sets switched on we could hear the voices of other breakers conversing about lost babies, prowling police cars, that afternoon's football fixtures. As we came off the Hammersmith Flyover the traffic was slowing down ahead of us. Richie's voice cut into the conversation between the mother of the lost baby and a taxi driver cruising in her area.

45

'On the side.'

'Ten four, goodbuddie,' the taxi driver answered. 'Break on the side and bring it in. What's your handle?'

'You've got Croesus here,' Richie said, using the code name we had agreed on. 'Spud, goodbuddie, are you on the side?'

'Yeh, you got me.'

'Go twenty-two.'

'Roger D.' I switched to Channel 22. It seemed to be clear of interference. 'On channel.'

'Not much chance to put the Audi through its paces in this. Somebody's probably pranged at the Hogarth Roundabout.'

'We won't have time to go to Isleworth now. I'll take Bill Garland his seventy grand on the way back from the airport. I can load the spares into the Saab at the same time.'

'Ten four, Spud, but watch it. This is not a private line, you know. I'll go breaker break and catch you later.'

I bit my lip. I had committed the cardinal sin of talking about a sensitive subject on an open radio.

'We gone, then.'

'Ten four.'

THREE

The Military Vehicle Engineering Establishment was near Addlestone, just alongside the M3. Designed for testing military vehicles, it had an outer circuit like a race track, a "mountain" section, various stretches of excessively unkind surfaces and a loop of rough road very similar to a rally stage.

We reached the swing gates at MVEE a few minutes before time. No RAOC vehicle had yet shown up. Tro betrayed her readiness to use feminine charm when it suited her by persuading the uniformed custodian to let her take the Audi out onto the track. There were no tanks on test at that moment. The drivers had knocked off for lunch.

She beckoned me across to the Quattro and I strapped myself into the passenger's seat with the competition-style safety harness. She gripped the steering wheel confidently and we drove out onto the empty outer circuit. I was all right while she did a few laps of the two-and-a-half mile oval-shaped track, taking the car to its maximum of 140 mph. Even when she peeled off onto the mountain circuit and tested the car's traction on the tight bends my stomach behaved, though the sideways G-forces were enormous. But when she took to the rough loop with its pot-holes and gritty surface I began to pray that I would nct throw up. Stones rattled against the wheel arches like machine-gun fire and I was thrown from side to side, only restrained by the harness.

She was getting the hang of the car, discovering that with four wheel drive and both differentials locked she could go for a corner without taking up the sideways attitude used by rally drivers of normal cars. She could also come out of bends faster.

'Great!' she shouted at me above the din. 'Even if I, you know, lift off or brake in a corner the dynamic balance of tyre forces remains the same, I mean on all four wheels.'

47

'Oops!'

The exception proves the rule and at that instant she'd overdone it. A friendly bush collected us. Tro said, 'Shit,' selected first gear and drove out of the mire.

When we rejoined Richie and Clement a small Army truck, bearing RAOC markings had drawn up alongside the Saab. Clement was talking to a Captain wearing a khaki pullover with leather shoulder patches. He was a studious type with spectacles and a long, somewhat doleful face. In his hand was a clipboard to which three sheets of paper were fastened.

'Captain Drummond,' Clement introduced us. 'Patrick Malone.'

Tro had opened the bonnet of the Audi and was bending over the engine.

'This is all very irregular,' Captain Drummond said. Like all quartermasters he was jealous of his stores. 'I've never issued any of this equipment to civilians but — ' he shrugged, 'I've had instructions direct from Logistics Executive at Andover.'

He looked at Richie and me uncertainly and cast a nervous glance at Tro's bejeaned posterior. My appearance was hardly military but Richie, with his quarter-deck manner and general air of battles past, seemed to reassure him.

'Corporal Ames, will you unload the items as I read them out.'

'Yes, sir.' They were the only words I heard the driver speak. He jumped down from his seat and, whistling soundlessly, let down the tailboard of the truck.

'First, two AR 10 Armalites.'

Corporal Ames reached into the van and produced two rifles. They had cooling vents along the barrel and a skeleton metal stock.

'These have been sleeved down to take .223 ammo,' Drummond explained. 'The .223 has less recoil than the standard 7.62 millimetre, so it's more accurate on automatic. The metal stock folds back on the gun when not in use, i.e. in a vehicle.'

'Are all the parts metal?' Richie asked.

48

'Only the stock, fore-end and pistol grip. The rest is a plastic material. I've given you six magazines and two hundred rounds of ammo. These rounds have a fat cartridge. Gives a muzzle velocity of 32 f.p.s.' Drummond moved his finger to the second item on his list. 'Item two, one telescopic sight and one image-intensifying sight. Three, a roll of Cortex and six detonators. You know how to use it? Put a rectangle of this against a wall and it'll blow out a door for you.'

Corporal Ames was handing the items to Clement. Clement checked each one before putting it on the platform below the open hatch-back of the Saab. The Cortex looked like a coil of thick electric wiring cable.

'Four, six Browning 9 millimetre Hi-power pistols, plus twelve thirteen-round magazines and a hundred rounds of ammo. Five, one Winchester 12-bore pump gun. This is the weapon used by the US police.'

The Corporal produced a wicked-looking gun. Its length was only a couple of inches over two feet and it had a thick cylinder below the barrel.

'How does that thing work?'

'It's operated by pumping the magazine. You have five rounds. Every time you pump you get one in the chamber. With this you can spray the entire wall of a room with shot at twenty feet.'

'You know this gun, Clem?'

Clement nodded. 'Blasting locks off doors.'

'Six, a box of twelve concussion grenades and detonators. Some people call them stun grenades. Mostly noise, but effective.'

Drummond's spectacles had slid a few millimetres down his nose. He used his right index finger to push them up again, then returned it to the clipboard.

'Seven, two Mach 10 Ingram hand-guns. Useful in close quarter work. It fires 9 mm parabellum at twenty rounds per second. Cuts a man in half.'

Corporal Ames gingerly handed over a squat weapon with a short barrel and square magazine.

'Now we come to the specialised items.' The RAOC Captain folded the first sheet over the top of his board. 'Item eight is a set of thermal sensors. You know these? They locate human presence by body warmth.'

Clement nodded and Richie assumed a wise expression.

'Nine, two pairs of image-intensifying goggles. These are the latest pattern. I won't give you the spec because that's classified.'

'Degree of intensification?'

'Bright moonlight,' Drummond replied. 'That's in conditions of maximum darkness. Okay?'

His head jerked round as Tro slammed the bonnet of the Audi shut. She lay down on the ground and wriggled half under the car to examine the front suspension. Drummond contemplated her for a moment with a puzzled frown, then returned to his list.

'Now, this last item is a bit special. I was lucky to get hold of one for you. They're still top secret. It's the Mark 3 audio-visual monitor TV with sound attachment.'

'Mark 3?' Clement said. 'I know the Mark 1 and 2.'

'This is a great improvement. The flexible tubing contains an optic fibre with a fish-eye lens at the end, and also the lead to a micro spike mike. They feed back to a small TV screen and sound amplifier. The drill, rods and battery are in this case. And that's the lot. Ten items in all.'

Corporal Ames put up the tailboard of the truck and Captain Drummond tucked his clipboard under his arm.

'Suppose you want a signature for all this,' Clement said, with a faint smile.

'No. This stuff has been written off. We don't expect to see any of it again.' Captain Drummond shook his head despairingly. 'Lord knows what the Treasury will say if they ever get to hear of this. Must be at least twenty thousand pounds worth of stuff there.'

Now that he had parted with the equipment Captain Drummond was in a hurry to make his escape. Before they remounted their vehicle both he and the Corporal saluted Richie. God alone knew who they thought he was, but the salute was proof that even during the short meeting he had managed to exert his usual force and authority.

Tro and Clement headed back towards London with the Audi Quattro. Richie settled into the passenger seat of the Saab beside me. Our next stop was Heathrow Airport. The time was 12.40. Richie's flight to Geneva was due to take off at 1.15.

'It's up to you to get this show on the road, Pat.' We were crossing the bridge over the M3, heading north towards Staines. 'I don't like having to go off like this but it's absolutely vital to fix up the money side of this job. You'd better let Tro drive the Quattro. That'll keep her happy. Apart from that it's up to you who goes with you. Pick me up at the Beau Rivage Hotel. It's near the Pont Mont Blanc. You should be there well before midnight.'

'Assuming we're not in prison at Calais.'

'You can camouflage this stuff with the spares you pick up from Bill Garland. It's the guns and ammo that might be awkward. I wouldn't like to try and smuggle them into the UK, but the French and Italian Customs are usually pretty easy on private cars. And I think your cover of being a rally crew will do the trick, especially with the Italians. If you do get held up anywhere along the line ring Nick. We can use him as a report centre.'

It had become a habit with me to monitor the traffic on the road behind me. I noticed the black Ford Capri as we came through the tunnel that links the airport terminal buildings with the A4 and M4. It was still three cars behind me as I went up the curving ramp that leads to the departure doors at Terminal One.

Richie tipped the seat forward to collect his bag from the rear. He had just fifteen minutes in which to catch his 'plane.

'See you in Geneva, then. What's the matter?'

He'd noticed that I was staring into the mirror. The Ford Capri had stopped by the kerb fifty yards back. No one was getting out.

'Don't look back,' I said, 'but I'm wondering about a car that's been behind us coming through the tunnel.'

'I'll have to leave that problem to you, old pal. You'll just have to lose him, won't you?'

He slammed the door, gave me a wave and disappeard through the automatic doors.

I drove sedately back through the tunnel. The Ford Capri was still three cars behind me. We emerged from the tunnel, negotiated the roundabout and entered the mile-long stretch of dual carriageway leading to the motorway. I kept my speed down, not exceeding 60 mph, but sticking to the middle lane. Every other private car was doing at least the legal maximum, passing me in the fast lane or flashing me from behind to move over. The Ford Capri kept his distance.

The test would be the roundabout at the end of the stretch. If he was really following me he would move closer as we approached it.

He did.

As an additional test I made a complete circuit of the roundabout under the motorway, ignoring all the exits. He stayed with me.

Instead of heading back into town I took the road westward. Once up on the motorway I checked for police cars, then put my foot down. Even with the load and the extra weight of the bullet-proofing the turbocharged Saab could accelerate rapidly to her top speed of 125 mph. The Capri was able to match me.

That meant it was one of the 2.8 injection models and I had a problem. I could see two heads in the front seats and another in the back.

How and why had I picked up a tail? Since when had he been following? If I'd been in the Quattro I'd have guessed it was some enthusiast anxious to prove his car against it. But the Saab Turbo was no longer an unusual car.

The first exit for Slough was coming up fast. The various possibilities were racing through my mind equally fast.

The Army's security was not always as good as it might be. My tail could have latched onto the ROAC vehicle on its way from the depot and waited to pick us up as we came out of the MVEE. Equally possible was that my indiscretion on the CB had been picked up and had aroused someone's interest. I had mentioned the airport, the Saab and the seventy grand in the same breath. At this moment the Saab was well worth hijacking. I was reluctant to face the possibility that the news of our assignment had leaked. Surely not *already*. It was only eight hours since Richie had accepted Charles's brief. But if the worst had happened my pursuers could be anything from Red Brigades "brothers" in London to the KGB itself.

One thing was certain. I could not go back into London till I had disposed of them.

I peeled off into the slow lane at the last possible moment before the Slough exit, went into the roundabout and made a sharp left. That brought me, in a few hundred yards, onto the old Colnbrook By-Pass, a lethal road with only three lanes for both east and west-bound traffic. I leaned forward and flicked up an extra switch that I'd had fitted. It disconnected the brake lights — an old trick used by criminals fleeing from the police.

He realised now I'd spotted him and had moved closer. That meant the occupants of the car were working alone. If they had been part of a co-ordinated team they would have peeled off at the roundabout and let another car take over the tail. It also meant that they had a heist in mind.

I was studying the traffic coming the other way. When I saw a gap of three hundred yards or so I moved over to the right-hand side of the road, changing into a lower gear. When the alignment of the car was straight I prodded the accelerator with my right foot and trod on the brakes with my left. At the same instant I wrenched the steering wheel clockwise. The car spun through a half circle. As it completed the 180 degrees I took my foot off the brake to stop the spin. I dropped another gear and accelerated hard. It's the technique for brake-turning a Saab and I'd practised it regularly. You can't do an ordinary hand-brake turn because the hand-brake operates on all four wheels.

The Capri, taken by surprise and crowded by the vehicles behind it, shot past on my right. Cars coming up on my side were hooting and flashing. The leading car had braked and the others were double-banking. I heard a succession of thudding crashes behind me as a nasty accident built up. The Capri was caught up in it. He'd had no chance to emulate my manoeuvre, even if he had the nerve and skill to do it.

Using the full boost of the compressor I bombed up the central lane, forcing laggard vehicles out of my path. I went round the same roundabout on the limit of adhesion and rejoined the London-bound carriageway of the M4. There was no sign of any black Ford Capri behind me as I drove at maximum speed towards London, with headlights flashing to ward interlopers off my fast lane.

I made a detour to Isleworth, where I handed Bill Garland his seventy grand and collected the spares he had put together for me. In the privacy of his garage I used them to camouflage the equipment which we'd collected from the ROAC Captain. Dismantled into their three main component parts the Armalites were not difficult to conceal. The barrels fitted inside spare exhaust pipes, the remaining parts rubbed shoulders inconspicuously with the pistons, gear assemblies, springs, and so on which Bill had provided. The Brownings fitted snugly into the botton tray of a metal toolbox.

The cartons from CCS looked conspicuous. I decided to unpack the toys Richie had bought and let them take their chance with the other equipment. His shopping list had consisted of a B-409 telephone tap alert set, a CS11 covert camera spy system, a couple of bug alerts — one small enough to attach to a digital wrist-watch — two body-shield waistcoats and two body-shield field jackets. There was also a CCX-1000 bomb-detector, intended primarily for checking cars.

The boot of the Saab was a right jumble when I'd packed everything in with a selection of spare parts uppermost. As an afterthought I asked Bill to throw in a couple of his green team overalls and a pair of crash helmets.

Back at the flat I found the five remaining members of what Richie called his squad sampling hot garlic bread, cheese and pâté. Johnnie, the gourmet, had found time to pay a visit to Harrods Food Hall. Stan had come back from Sandfords with a complete set of the Touring Club Italiano 1:200,000 maps.

'You've been a hell of a time,' Tro commented. 'We've been back over half an hour.'

'There was a traffic jam in the Heathrow tunnel.' I'd decided not to say anything about the Capri. I'd had time to think and I felt I might have over-reacted. 'What's the form on road conditions, Stan?'

'Straightforward to Dover except for a mile of single-lane traffic near Chatham. Weather forecast is not good but ferry and services are okay. No need to book, they have plenty of space. I rang a pal of mine in the Kent police. He came out to Rhodesia with Lord Soames just before Independence. He's going to tell their motorway patrols not to worry if they see a red, white and blue Audi and a Saab Turbo exceeding the limit. I gave him the numbers.'

Stan was pleased with himself. I did not point out that there could be disadvantages in having our registration numbers logged by the police. Stan's information would probably go into the Police National Computer, and access to the PNC was not as restricted as it should be.

Nick appeared to be more out of things than ever. The rest of the group were not blatantly cold-shouldering him. It was just that no-one spoke to him. I saw Johnnie studying him covertly, as if he was trying to read his thoughts.

The last thing we did before going down to the cars was listen to a news bulletin.

The crisis over Russian activities on the Polish frontier had intensified. The President of the United States had even gone so far as to use the satellite link — the hot line — to talk to the President of the Soviet Union. We seemed to be teetering on the brink of the ultimate calamity. The item on General Stewart added nothing to what we knew already. The Prime Minister, questioned in Parliament, had expressed the Government's confidence in the ability of the Italian Government to deal with the matter. No, the anti-terrorist unit of the SAS would *not* be despatched, the Italians had their own special police for just such eventualities. On the A4 two men had been killed in a multiple accident. Their car, a Ford Capri, had been in collision with a van. The third passenger and the driver of the van were seriously ill in hospital. Police were anxious to question the driver of a . . .

I switched the set off. It was five minutes past two and time for us to go. Ten hours after Richie had first 'phoned me we went down to the cars, now parked outside the flat. We each had a small grip or shoulder-satchel with the bare essentials, no more. Nick was left to guard the fort.

I had a good look round the Square before getting into the Saab. There was no sign of loiterers, betraying by their body language that they were covertly observing us, no cars with occupants sitting in the front seats waiting. Clement and Stan joined me. Johnnie was going to ride with Tro.

I had already pulled away from the kerb when she flashed her lights at me. Johnnie was getting out of the car again. In the mirror I saw him go back into the building. I pulled into a parking space a hundred yards on.

I reached for the CB mike. We were still on Channel 22. 'Hello, Speedy Lady. Spud calling. What's the hold up?'

'No problem, Spud,' Tro's voice came back. 'He's left his wallet in the flat.'

'Stupid berk!'

We lost five minutes waiting for him. He showed no trace of contrition when he came out again, just gave me a cheery wave and slid into his seat.

Checking in my mirror that Tro was following, I drove round Melton Square and then turned south towards the river. When I came to the King's Road the traffic lights were red. I was waiting for them to change when a police car came blaring along from the direction of Chelsea Town Hall. Its lights were flashing, siren screaming. It rocked round the front of the Saab, missing it by a foot.

In the back seat Stan twisted round to watch it. The lights changed to green. I let in the clutch.

Stan reached for the mike. He was quickly picking up Citizen Band jargon. 'Got your ears on, Speedy Lady? Ex-Colonial calling. Did you see where the Smokies went?'

It was Johnnie's voice that came back. 'I got you, Goodbuddie. Think they turned into Melton Square.'

56

In convoy we took the South Circular round to the M20. Every now and then I'd get several cars ahead of Tro but she always closed up quickly. She knew the route. It was the way to Brands Hatch circuit. Soon we were bowling along the motorway at a nice 120. Tro sat on my tail ten yards back as if she were slipstreaming me.

Before Maidstone a Jaguar came up very fast from behind us and flashed. We moved over. He went past, the plain-clothes man in the passenger seat checking the occupants of both cars carefully. Then he in his turn moved over and waved us on.

At junction 7 we jinked off the M20 to travel north-east for six miles and join the M2. We had resumed our normal gait of two miles per minute when a Mercedes-Benz 500 SL, piqued at being overtaken, tried to join the party. The unmarked police car must have been shadowing us from behind. After a few miles it came storming up and signalled the Merc into the emergency lane. Most unfair.

The last ten miles of the A2 into Dover were slow. We were balked by bunches of juggernaut lorries moving to and from the Channel ferries. It had started to rain hard and each vehicle was surrounded by a shroud of spray. Side winds buffeted the car whenever we came out from under the lee of one of these monsters.

We reached the terminal at Dover to find that departures had been suspended because of the bad weather in the Channel. I made a call to Charles on the number he had given Richie. He must have put pressure on some top executive at Hoverspeed. After an hour's delay the service was resumed and we were waved on at the head of the queue of waiting vehicles. Johnnie had taken advantage of the opportunity to remove the magnetic aerials from the roof and conceal them in the boot. Our CB rigs were legal in the UK but illegal on the Continent.

Ten minutes later the four Proteus gas-turbine engines were started, we ballooned up and slid off the sloping ramp.

I said to Johnnie: 'You got your wallet all right?'

He gave me a blank stare. 'My wallet?'

'Tro said you left it in the flat.'

'Oh, yes. I got it.' The smile again creased his face. 'No problem.'

Outside the harbour the sea was rough and a gale was blowing. The noise was deafening and the craft was surrounded by spray, visibility nil.

We were half-way across when Tro got up from her seat. She caught my eye and gave a jerk of her head. As she headed for the loos I followed her, clinging to seat backs and hand-rails to keep my balance.

Though there was no pitching the noise and the buffeting were having their effect on Stan. He felt so ill that he had to lie flat on a row of seats, with the prettiest of the stewardesses ministering to him. Johnnie, oblivious to the conditions, was trying to chat up the second stewardess. He had to bawl his pleasantries at the top of his voice.

Tro waited for me outside the Ladies.

'When we get to Calais can you take Johnnie and give me someone else?'

'What's the matter? Did he want to have it off with you?'

She gave me a look of scorn. 'He's an odd-ball. I don't know what he went back to the flat for. I mean, it wasn't to fetch his wallet.'

She had her mouth close to my ear. The tang of the garlic bread was still on her breath.

'How do you know?'

'Something happened up there. I got a, you know, very funny feeling from him. I mean, he was sort of drained. If it wasn't ridiculous I'd have said he'd been wanking himself. And his B.O. Phew, it's strong!'

'All right. Clem can go with you. I'll tell Johnnie I want to discuss these CB — '

'Not Clem. He's a cold bloody fish.'

'That only leaves Stan.'

'Stan will do. I don't mind Stan.'

It was a relief to reach the calmer water near the French shore. The French police and customs officers did not question our story about being a rally car and service vehicle.

58

After a glance at the jumble in the boot of the Saab they waved us on and went back to their Gauloises, *pastis* and cards.

Owing to the bad weather the crossing had taken fifty instead of the usual thirty-five minutes. In addition, we had lost another hour through no fault of our own. French time was an hour ahead of British. It was 5.40. Geneva was a thousand kilometres away.

Stan recovered quickly from his sea-sickness. He was visibly tickled by the idea of riding with Tro. In my heart I wished him joy. Johnnie made no demur about swopping to the Saab. Clement took a turn in the back seat, sitting sideways to accommodate his long legs. Johnnie sat beside me.

'Seat belt,' I reminded him.

'Sod that.'

'It's required by law in France.'

Reluctantly he fastened the belt across his ample stomach.

By six o'clock we were on the newly-extended A1 autoroute. We had no friendship with the traffic police, but at a steady 125 mph — 200 kilometres an hour — we were not over-conspicuous. Plenty of other cars were travelling at that speed.

Paris is 300 kilometres from Calais. We reached the Boulevard Périphérique at 7.15. Circling Paris was slow but not as slow as if we'd arrived at the *heure de pointe* an hour or two earlier. By 7.45 we were again on the fast motorway, but a lot of traffic was moving out of Paris. Our progress consisted of bursts up to 120 mph and then enforced dawdles at 80. Gradually the traffic thinned as motorists peeled off into the suburbs. By the time we passed the exit for Fontainebleau we had resumed our normal tempo of a couple of miles a minute. It was 8.15 and Paris was forty miles behind us.

We had decided on the hovercraft to use Autoroute all the way, accepting the longer loop via Lyon, Chambéry and Annecy, rather than cut across country from Macon to Geneva. That way the two capitals are 408 miles apart.

We rolled into Geneva and over the Pont Mont Blanc at fifteen minutes past midnight. *Péages*, stops for petrol and the perfunctory Swiss Customs had knocked 20 mph off our average. I had not noticed Johnnie's B.O. Both he and Clement had dozed for most of the journey, making up for a lost night's sleep.

There was plenty of activity still at the Beau Rivage. Lush cars were parked outside its restaurant, Le Chat Botté, one of the few in Geneva to earn a star from the *Guide Michelin*.

After six hours in the cars it was a relief to stretch our legs. I had to dissuade Johnnie from going into the restaurant and sampling the *menu gastronomique*. We'd be moving on in a few minutes. I left him and the others to stamp about outside, admiring the spectacle of the mountains gleaming in the brilliant moonlight.

Richie was sitting in the foyer, talking to a beautiful Swiss woman with a very chic *coiffure* and a dress that bore the stamp of Yves St Laurent. He had evidently made a lot of headway with her. She pouted sadly when he told her that their time had run out. I had to wait while he saw her into a taxi, gallant up till the last hand-kiss.

'I expected you an hour ago,' he said, as he came back to rejoin me.

'You haven't been wasting your time.' I nodded at the departing taxi. 'An old flame?'

'She was good cover. One is always less conspicuous in the company of a woman than alone.' A debatable point when the woman is as striking as Richie's recent companion. 'What held you up?'

'You forgot about the hour's difference in time. I'd say we've done bloody well. There was a force ten gale blowing in the Channel. I had to ring up Charles. He got them to run a hovercraft specially for us.'

'You rang Charles? Did he mind?'

'He was a bit curt but he did his stuff.'

Richie was tense. He was studying the faces of the people coming in and out of the hotel.

'There was a car on your tail when you dropped me at Heathrow. What happened there?'

'I had to lose him, like you said. That took time.'

'Did he ever show up again?'

'No. I'm sure we were clean when we left the flat.'

Richie was watching a young, dark-skinned man who had come into the hotel and was wandering about vaguely. He appeared ill at ease in these luxurious surroundings.

'I've been trying to ring Nick. There's no reply. He was there when you left?'

'Yes.'

'Then why the hell doesn't he answer?'

'I must say I wondered how long Nick would be prepared to sit on his butt and answer 'phone calls. If this trip of ours was leaked he'd be at risk.'

'So would we. Even Nick could be persuaded to talk.'

'There was one funny thing — '

'Yes?'

'Just as we were leaving Johnnie went back to the flat. He said he'd forgotten his wallet.'

'Johnnie went back to the flat — alone?'

I nodded.

'*Jesus Christ!*'

Richie was looking at me but he wasn't seeing me. The nearest he ever came to showing emotion was the slight quivering of a muscle below his glass eye.

'Tro said she thought something had happened up there. Johnnie's manner was odd.'

Richie came back into focus. 'This is something that will have to wait till tomorrow. Right now all I want is to get out of here. I've felt like a sore thumb hanging around for you.'

'Were you being watched?'

'You can't always tell. Anyone with a hundred grand on him is apt to feel exposed. I'd like to off-load some of the money on you people before the Italian Customs. I have two hundred million in lire. There's a credit of another three thousand million waiting for us at the Bank of Rome.'

The dark-skinned man had located the Toilette and homed on it. He must have come in from the street searching for a free piddle.

'There's a limit on the amount of currency you can take into Italy.'

'I know. But have you ever actually been searched?'

Geneva is in a little tongue of Switzerland that probes the flesh of France. The city is so French in character that the *Guide Michelin* has annexed it. We had entered Swiss territory a few miles before it and left a few miles outside it. Customs formalities were perfunctory.

We were on the autoroute until a few miles before Chamonix, where we came onto an ordinary *route nationale*. It was a winding road which offered magnificent panoramas — or would have in daylight. Roadworks had been carried out to straighten the highway. Some of the bends in the old road had been left as lay-bys for motorists who wanted to stop and feast their eyes. At Richie's direction I pulled into one of these D-shaped loops. No other cars were there. As I parked, the Quattro nosed up a couple of feet behind me.

The moon had gone behind cloud as we dismounted for Richie's share-out. In the darkness I felt a sense of emptiness beyond the low wall defining the curve of the D. The road must fall away steeply from the other side. A stony bank screened us from the passing traffic. A hundred yards back down the road a car had stopped and switched off its lights.

Richie used the boot-lid of the Saab as a counter. He slapped his leather pouch on it and unfastened the zip. We stood in a half-circle on the wall side of the cars, like dogs waiting for the master to feed us. The side-lights of the Audi provided a shadowy illumination.

The Italian currency was bulky. He had it divided up already into six separate bundles.

'I'm going to give you each a million for immediate expenses. We'll split the rest into two lots and stash half in each car.'

'What's a million lire worth?' Stan wanted to know.

'About four hundred pounds. It's up to you how you carry it but I suggest you keep it on your person. They seldom do a body-search.'

We each took our bundle. I folded mine into a square pad and zipped it into the breast-pocked of the anorak I was wearing.

Richie was just pulling out the two bigger bundles when our whole group was brilliantly illuminated. A car coming fast up the road without lights had suddenly switched on its headlamps and veered into the lay-by. At first I thought a linkage had broken in the steering. But the driver had his car fully under control. It slid to a halt across the bows of the Saab.

Even before it had come to rest a second car also switched on headlamps, swung into the lay-by and rocked to a halt behind the Audi.

In that instant of shocked surprise I was aware of a quick movement beside me. Clement had put his right hand inside his jacket.

The two doors on the nearside of each of the cars had been flung open. Four men came out, crouching. Their shapes were picked out starkly by the headlamps, like figures on a stage lit only by footlights. One of them was holding a sub-machine gun. The other three had pistols. Their faces were black shadows under crew cuts.

'Up your 'ands,' the man with the sub-machine gun ordered us in bad English. 'Come out from be'ind the cars. Slow, or I put a burst in the girl.'

We were covered and unarmed, our weapons still in the boot of the Saab.

Even before I had time to put my hands up I was deafened by two shots from close to my ear. The sub-machine gunner buckled. Six more shots went off — *bang-bang* . . . *bang-bang* . . . *bang-bang*.

The three remaining gun-men jerked and fell. Only one of them managed to get off a shot. It hit the wall and went zinging into the night. The whole thing had happened in less than five seconds.

My head jerked round. I saw Clement's forearms on the roof of the Saab, the left hand supporting the right. He was gripping a Browning automatic. I had just time to register a quick mental photograph of him in that posture before he moved. He walked deliberately between the Saab and the

Audi, covering the open doors of our visitors' cars. They were both empty.

Still holding his pistol ready, he checked the four bodies lying in the roadway. None of them moved. All four had been drilled through the heart.

I was shocked into immobility. It was the first demonstration I'd seen of reflex SAS marksmanship.

'Christ, Clem — !' Even Richie had been stunned by the speed and violence of the incident. 'They might be police.'

Tro swayed and leaned against me. I put an arm round her back to hold her.

'Not police.' Clement nodded at the sub-machine gun which had clattered from the spokesman's hands. 'An Uzi. Swiss police don't use 'em.'

Richie went to one of the corpses, pulled the head round to examine the face.

'Come here, Patrick.'

I went across and looked down at the horribly grimacing face. It was the dark-skinned man who had been looking for the loo in the Beau Rivage. Richie thrust a hand inside his jacket and pulled the wallet out. With it came an Italian passport and a work permit for Switzerland.

'Stan, make sure no-one else drives into this lay-by.' For the moment Clement was in charge. He spoke in a quiet, matter-of-fact voice. 'Johnnie, help me get these beauties back in their cars. We'll drive them over the edge.'

'Okay, Richie?' Johnnie looked to Richie for confirmation.

Richie was slapping his hands on the 10,000 lire notes, which a sudden breeze was threatening to blow away. He did not answer Johnnie's query right away.

'Who do you suppose they were, Pat?'

'Anyone see you withdrawing that money from the bank?'

'I guess so. You think they were just bandits?'

'Who knows?'

'It's a bloody nuisance. If we report this we'll be in Switzerland till Doomsday. *Damn*! Okay, Clem. That's the only thing we can do.'

I joined the burial party. Between us, Johnnie, Clement

and I lugged the bodies back into the cars, one behind each steering wheel. All the time vehicles were racing past on the road twenty yards away. One motorist tried to come into our lay-by. We froze, pinioned by his headlamps.

Stan made no signals, just stood in his way, starting to undo his flies. The motorist backed out and drove on up the road.

'Did he see anything?'

'Don't think so. Too much shadow.'

I put on the driving gloves I'd left on the shelf above the Saab's dashboard and went to deal with the foremost car, a Renault. There was a gap at the end of the parapet where a hedge met the wall. Beyond it sure enough the ground fell away sheer. The Renault was an automatic, no problem. I started the engine, opened the bonnet and increased the idling speed. I lowered the window on the driver's side, reached in and pulled the quadrant to the Drive position. The car began to creep forward. I closed the door. Walking beside it, I put a hand through the window onto the steering wheel to guide the bonnet towards the gap.

When it was nicely aimed I stood back and watched it go.

It brushed the hedge aside, then nose-dived into the darkness. I heard it thumping and bumping its way down the incline. When there came a silence I thought it had stopped rolling. A second later a bigger crash came echoing up. Deeper than I'd thought. But no explosion, no flames.

Clement had watched what I'd done and did the same with the Peugeot. He didn't ask to borrow my gloves. If he wanted to leave fingerprints on the steering wheel that was his privilege.

Cars and occupants had vanished from our lives, leaving only four pools of blood on the tarmac to show they had ever existed.

FOUR

'Where did you get that gun, Clem?' Richie asked.

'It's my own Browning. I never move without it.'

'Suppose you're searched at Customs?'

'It's a chance I'm prepared to take. That's why I never travel by air.'

I'd come across men who were like that. Men who had stayed alive because of the gun and now they could not live without it.

'If the Italians search you it'll be all up with this whole party.'

'It'll be all up anyway if they search.' The Browning had gone back into its holster in the crook of Clement's arm. He had no intention of parting with his weapon.

Richie did not insist.

We all wanted to be away from that place without delay. Very little was said as we stashed the remaining currency in the Saab and Audi. Even Johnnie had been sobered by what had happened. Those cars had not gone down into the valley silently. Even now some French citizen might be telephoning the police. The frontier was seven miles away. We had to get across it before an alert was raised.

This was where the play-acting had to begin. Tro and I would take the Quattro as driver and co-driver. Richie prevailed on us to wear the green overalls that I'd won from Bill Garland.

'You all right, Tro?'

I'd noticed that she'd wobbled standing on one leg to get the overalls on. Her face was chalky white.

She steadied when she got into the driving seat with the familiar feel of the wheel in her hands. We started on the last few miles to the Mont Blanc tunnel, which joins France to Italy.

The officials on "the Blonk" are more interested in heavy lorries than in private cars moving from one European Community country to the other. Tro was slowing down at the French post when a gendarme in a képi spotted the British registration number and waved us on. The Saab close behind was given the same treatment. A moment later we had entered the black maw of the tunnel.

It is usually a hell on earth, full of fumes, noise and dazzling lights. The mastodon shapes of the juggernauts can be alarming in that reverberating gloom. Even at three o'clock in the morning there was a stream of heavy lorries moving both ways.

There was no light at the end of the tunnel. Tro was taken by surprise as we emerged and found ourselves face to face with the Italian customs.

This was the big test. It is important not to feel nervous when you're smuggling. Customs men can pick up the scent of guilt. Apart from the Italian currency, the Audi was innocent enough. I tried not to think of the guns and ammunition in the Saab.

The Italian *Guardia di Finanza* were interested all right. As soon as they saw the Audi's rally livery and its decoration of advertising decals they converged on it. When they discovered that it had a young woman as driver they became even more enthusiastic. And, she spoke Italian!

The conversation soon became technical. When Tro got out of the car I thought they had asked to inspect the boot, but it was the bonnet she had opened. They wanted to see the engine.

Five cylinders? *Ma, Come mai?*

The inspection went on for five minutes. One of the Customs men even lay on the ground to examine the *retrotreno*.

'*I pezzi di ricambio sono nell'altra macchina,*' Tro explained.

Richie had thrown up the hatch-back of the Saab without invitation so that they could see the mountain of spares. The *Guardia* were more interested in the four bottles of Johnny Walker lying on top of the pile. Two of them changed hands

67

and the hatch-back was closed.

Then we were waved on with cries of *avanti*! *avanti*! and exhortations to step on it. Tro obliged and took off with all four wheels leaving black streaks on the road surface. But I noticed that her driving had lost its edge. Her line on some of the fast, sweeping bends was untidy.

We had only gone a few kilometres when she slowed and pulled into a lay-by. Even before the car had stopped she was undoing her seat-belt.

'I'm going to be sick.'

Just in time she got the car door open and puked onto the verge. She retched for a while, then sat back, gasping. It was delayed reaction from the shock of the shooting display. She had probably never seen corpses or the terrible violence of killing before. I knew she needed a face-saver.

'It's those ham sandwiches we bought on the autoroute. I thought they were stale at the time.'

'Yes.' Burp. 'Ham never did agree with me.'

'Shall I drive for a while?'

'Yup.'

Unsteadily she climbed out and we exchanged places. As I readjusted the seat, the Saab pulled in behind us. Johnnie got out and went to the back to open the boot. I saw him coming towards the Audi with the magnetic aerial in his hand. There was a clunk as he placed it on the roof. I opened the door so that he could re-connect the leads to the rig.

'Everybody okay here?' he said, with a quick glance at Tro's pale face.

'Couldn't be better.'

'Stay on channel, Goodbuddie.'

I closed the door and engaged first gear. The thirty miles of road from the Mont Blanc tunnel down to Aosta is a lovely stretch for a driver, even in the dark. The Audi, with the exceptional traction of its four-wheel drive, was able to take the curves flat out. The lights of the Saab fell further and further back.

Now that she'd been sick Tro recovered quickly.

'That was murder, wasn't it?'

'Clem, you mean?'

'Yes.'

'Or self-defence. It could have been *our* bodies pushed over into the valley.'

'But if they only wanted the money — '

'We don't know that. It was too much of a coincidence that one of them was a guest-worker from Italy.'

'How could anyone have known we were going to be on that road?'

'There may have been a leak.'

'You mean — we have a mole?'

'Not necessarily. Someone may have been indiscreet. And we did blaze quite a trail coming out of the UK.'

She adjusted the facia ventilator to bring a cool breeze onto her face. She was still pulling in deep breaths.

'Wasn't Clem taking a big chance? Suppose he'd missed one of them.'

'He's an SAS marksman. They are deadly at that range. They're trained to account for five targets in three seconds. It's the double-tap system. Two rounds for each man.'

'Jesus!'

'Amateurs. They thought they were invincible because they had a fistful of gun. They came up against a professional.'

I sounded too complacent, even to myself. But it was true. Clement had taken a very big chance. He had reacted as if we were an SAS patrol ambushed by guerrillas in the Yemen. There would be a full-scale hunt when the French police discovered that the four bodies in those cars had been shot with 9 mm bullets from the same Browning.

In both cars we had our CB rigs switched on and we could hear Italian breakers chatting and joking with each other. But we kept off the air. I'd decided to keep the CBs for emergency use and not attract attention to ourselves by idle chatter. I'd learned the hard way how easily a vital piece of information could be picked up by a silent listener.

At Aosta, Richie closed up on us before we picked up the autostrada which would carry us to Rome. As we pushed through the night, headlamps slashing the darkness, I could see the mountains flanking the Val d'Aosta. On one side the moonlight cast deep shadows, on the other the gleaming snow-covered peaks reached up towards a spangled sky.

I said: 'The Matterhorn is in there somewhere — on our left.'

There was no reply. I glanced round and saw that Tro's head had slumped.

Milan, 184 kilometres on, came up at 4.30. We stopped to fill up with petrol. Tro woke up, feeling better. She was satisfied now that I could keep the car moving fast. She let me stay at the wheel.

The 211 kilometres to Bologna took an hour and a quarter. During that time Tro, lulled into confidences by the hum of the tyres and the rushing of the wind, gave me an unexpected glimpse of her past life.

Her parents' divorce had made her the rope in a "tug of love" when she was only five. She had been educated at a succession of international schools, following her Italian step-father from one Euratom plant to another. He had shown no real interest in her until her womanhood began to develop. Then he started to paw her in a way that revolted her. Her International Baccalaureate won her a place at the London School of Economics but she'd opted out after a year; the male students were disgusting. For six months she'd joined a commune, squatting in a Victorian house in Balham. Then came the windfall. Her natural father died a widower in Melbourne and bequeathed her his entire worldly possessions. The money had enabled her to get a footing in Formula Three motor racing. Her natural talent had done the rest.

There was not much on the autostrada and in fifth gear the engine note was subdued enough for me to hear her talking. The Italians respect fast drivers. They moved over quickly in response to my flashing headlamps, letting our two cars streak imperiously down the fast lane.

At Bologna the road swung towards the Appenines. The next hundred kilometre stretch was comparatively slow, with its more acute curves, frequent tunnels and enormous arcing viaducts. Day was breaking as we descended towards the Florentine plain.

Richie's voice came over on the CB. We'd been keeping contact on Channel 34. It wasn't used by the Italians but with their big amplifiers they were bleeding over from other channels.

'Spud, got your ears on?'

'Yeah, I'm, here, goodbuddie.'

'We all need a ten one hundred. Stop at the next motion lotion.'

'Roger D.'

It was 6.40 when I pulled into a service area from which the dome of Florence Cathedral could be seen across the flat plain.

We had been driving for twelve hours and had covered the best part of a thousand miles.

As the cars could not be left unattended we went into the café in two relays, Johnnie, Tro and Stan first. Richie begrudged every moment we were at a standstill.

'Ten minutes,' he told them. 'Not a minute more.'

Wherever the Audi stopped it attracted interest, but in Italy more than ever. We soon had a small crowd around us, admiring the Quattro's garish colours and asking technical questions. Richie's cover plan for getting us into Italy was working too well now. We'd soon have to give the Audi a respray.

Richie and Clement did not say any more about the shooting incident. They'd had plenty of time to chew that rag on the run from the Mont Blanc tunnel. When Tro and Stan came out after ten minutes the three of us took our turn.

From the bar of the café we could see Johnnie in the restaurant just starting to tuck into a plate of ham and eggs. Standing up we drank a string of capuccinos and wolfed down a whole pile of Motta brioches.

Richie bought twenty *gettoni* from the barman, took them to a public telephone under its perspex cowl on the wall. I saw him dial, then put the receiver to his ear. From his expression and set lips I knew that he was still getting no reply.

71

He handed the *gettoni* back to the barman, received cash in return.

'*Damn*!'

'Don't forget it's only six o'clock in England,' I reminded him.

He was in a foul temper. Without answering he went into the restaurant to haul Johnnie out, almost by the scruff of the neck.

Our stop had taken thirty instead of the stipulated twenty minutes. Tro and Stan had saved time by getting the cars filled up while they waited.

The run to Rome was a doddle. 280 kilometres. We did it in a couple of hours. When we passed the *raccordo anulare*, the ring road round the city, Richie took the lead to guide us to Franco's place. He pushed southward along the Via Flaminia till he hit the Tiber, then followed the river's curves as far as Castel Sant' Angelo. I caught a momentary glimpse of the world's most famous dome at the end of the Via della Conciliazione, beyond the lobster-claw pincers of St Peter's Square. There were shoals of tourists on the move, tramping towards the Vatican in the morning sunlight. They seemed as remote as creatures on another planet.

The Saab crossed the Ponte Sant' Angelo and plunged into the maze of narrow streets between the river and Piazza Navona. This was a very ancient district. There was hardly room for cars to squeeze between houses and shops. It is difficult to creep unnoticed into any part of Rome. Our two-car convoy excited a great deal of interest before Richie made a hairpin bend, mounted a short incline and drove through the dark archway of a large square building. Beyond the archway was a cobbled courtyard where a huge jasmine spread green shade and a tired fountain splattered spring water over mossy-green steps.

Suddenly we had passed from the din and bustle of modern Rome into a small mediaeval oasis.

The cars were parked outside a doorway through which I could see piles of cases of wine bottles. A notice on the wall indicated that this was a depot for Franco Padovani's Roma-

Londra wine axis.

Franco had heard the rumble of the car engines, magnified by the enclosing walls of the palazzo. He came running down from his flat to meet us. Physically he was the same and was wearing the suit in which I had last seen him in Richie's London flat. But there was a subtle change. He had shed his English veneer and slipped back into his Italian skin. His movements and gestures, even the set of his face, had become more animated, more *nervoso*. Even his spectacles flashed more brightly.

'I don't know about anybody else,' Johnnie said, climbing out of the back of the Saab, 'but my first priority now is a shit, shave and shampoo.'

'Not till you've found a body-shop where we can have the Audi re-sprayed,' Richie told him.

'I reserved you two rooms in the Albergo Luna,' Franco said hurriedly. 'I guess you want to sleep. It's very simple but clean. Just round the corner in the little square there. They're doubles. I could not hire singles.'

Richie and I went up to the flat with Franco. Richie was carrying the telephone tap alert he had bought from CCS in South Audley Street.

The approach to Franco's flat was stark — through a dark hall paved with worn red flagstones and up a staircase with wrought-iron banisters. The air was musty and chill.

'Palazzo Mellini was once the residence of a Roman nobleman,' Franco explained as he led the way. 'It is said that from its windows Dante watched the pilgrims crossing the bridge to the Vatican and recorded that impression in his *Paradiso*. Of course in those days it was all fields between here and the Tevere.'

He stopped on the third floor and put his key in the lock of the solid, freshly-varnished oak door. The knocker had come from North Africa, a woman's hand enclosing a ball. The interior of the flat was a surprise, sumptuously furnished and crammed with pictures, statues, rugs, chandeliers, Etruscan *objets d'art*. The walls had been decorated in the Pompeiian style.

73

'This is my portfolio.' Franco smiled and waved a hand at his collection. 'The view from the sitting-room is quite something.'

Palazzo Mellini was on a small hill. From the added height of the third floor the windows looked out over the roofs of Rome. I could see the flattish dome of the Pantheon and the rust-coloured brick ruins on the Palatine Hill.

Richie was not interested in the history of the palace, nor the view.

'Have you made any progress, Franco?'

Franco passed a hand over his forehead. He looked even tireder than us.

'I arrived in Rome at five-fifteen yesterday evening. I have not slept since then. Rome is in a ferment. It is very difficult to find people. Some of them do not want to be found. Others are out of the city — '

He broke off. Richie had put his package on one of the brocaded chairs and was unpacking the telephone bug-alert.

'Did you find your contact in the special operations directorate — what's it called?'

'DIGOS. I tracked him to earth in the end. All police and military intelligence organisations are fully mobilised but they have come up with nothing.' Franco lifted one shoulder in an expressive shrug. 'Of course, there is much activity, but it is mainly to impress. House searches by NOCS and GIS squads, arrests, grilling of suspects and so on. But the truth is they have not one clue, though I guess there is a lot of screaming going on in the interrogation rooms.'

Franco had been out to buy every morning paper he could lay his hands on. They lay scattered all over the sitting-room.

'I have talked to a number of journalists. Several terrorist organisations are claiming they hold the General. They are all making demands on the Government — '

'What about his signet ring? Doesn't that prove *Colonna Nuova* have him?'

'But there is nobody to authenticate it. Not here in Rome.'

Richie extracted a compact, lidded box from its wrapping and stood it carefully on one of Franco's bow-legged tables.

'Has any reward been offered?'

'No. The Government has declared that it will not meet any of the kidnappers' demands.'

'That is where we may have an advantage.' Richie straightened up. 'I've arranged for a credit of three thousand million at the Banca di Roma. Two thousand million of that is available as a reward for information leading to the General's release. Your journalist friends would be the best way to leak that.'

Franco half shook his head, doubtful and unhappy. 'It is going to be dangerous. That can easily be traced back to me.'

'You can let it be known that you are acting on behalf of Lady Stewart. No-one is to know.'

'*Ma* — ' Franco pushed the spectacles back up his nose.

'Put it about, Franco. You've got a hundred million lire coming to you. And we're here to look after you. Where do you keep your 'phone?'

'Is better to 'phone from a public call-box, *magari un bar*.' In his agitation Franco's English was wearing thin. 'A many lines are being tapped because of this crisis.'

Richie patted the box he had unpacked. 'This meter will tell me if I'm being tapped. If it registers I promise you I'll ring off.'

While Richie did his 'phoning I collected my bag from the car and went into the bathroom for a wash and brush-up. I came out feeling a great deal better and smelling good, thanks to Franco's Paco Rabanne after-shave.

The moment I saw Richie I knew that something had gone seriously wrong.

'What's — '

He stopped me with a look and a warning nod of his head towards Franco.

'I've spoken to the Embassy,' he said in a low voice. 'The chap Charles gave me the name of. I think he's the undercover MI6 man there, though he passes for a Third Secretary. We're meeting him in Piazza Navona in half an hour.'

Down in the courtyard Stan had come back from the Albergo and was talking to Clement and Johnnie. A little

75

group of curious kids had collected round the Quattro. Franco was not the only inhabitant of the Palazzo. It had been split up to provide a dozen or so flats and maisonettes.

We went out through the archway and plunged into the narrow streets. It was not the first time that Richie had used Franco's place as a base. He knew his way round the Chiesa Nuova quarter. Piazza Navona was only ten minutes walk away.

'There was no reply from the flat again. I rang the Chelsea police station to ask them to go round and check up. When I gave them the address they asked me if I knew anyone called Nicholas Sheban Cantariu.'

'Nick's name?'

'It was. Before he fell off the balcony into the courtyard behind the flats.'

That stopped me in my tracks. 'He *fell* off the balcony?'

'As he wasn't resident there no one knew which flat he had come out of. They've been trying to check with all the missing owners since yesterday afternoon.'

'What did you say?'

'I disconnected. I'll say I was cut off. Eyetie operators.'

A three-wheeler Vespa with a miniature van on the back buzzed its horn at us angrily. We moved off the centre of the street.

'Since yesterday afternoon. When did it happen?'

'I didn't get that far.'

We turned left round a corner where a statue of the Madonna stood in a wall niche. A red light burned beneath it. The flowers in the little vase were fresh.

'Nick wasn't the kind of person who falls off balconies. Remember what you said when I told you Johnnie had gone back to the flat?'

Richie looked round at me. His face was grim. 'I picked Johnnie because he speaks Italian and he's a very tough fighter. But — if he thought Nick presented a danger to the job he'd take care of him.'

I remembered the strange feeling Tro had picked up from him. Drained, she said he was. And she'd smelled his body odour. Those could be the reactions of a man who had just geared himself up to kill.

'There's nothing to connect Nick with me,' Richie went on. 'He comes from Aberhosen. He wouldn't have told anyone at the Outward Bound school where he was going.'

I did not comment. Richie's anxiety not to be involved sounded callous. I gave him the benefit of the doubt and put it down to his concern not to compromise "the job".

I was still thinking about Nick and his strange manner just before we left him. I'd wondered at the time if he was thinking of shopping us. Now I was more inclined to believe it was a premonition of what was about to happen to him. A fall from a balcony was good cover. There might be other marks of violence on him but they would not be apparent on a body that had splashed onto concrete from the third floor.

'Are you going to say anything to Johnnie?'

He shook his head. 'What's the point? We have a job to do. I have to keep my squad together.'

The narrow street abruptly opened onto the spacious Piazza Navona, Rome's most companionable square. No cars were allowed here. The paved central area was occupied by street vendors. They had laid their wares out on the ground — garments, trinkets, leather goods. Romans walked slowly up and down in the oblique sunshine, conversing with eloquent gestures. It was odd in a city to hear the murmur of voices instead of the farting of traffic. A group of sight-seeing tourists had sat down on the circular rim of the central fountain. They were footsore already.

The buildings round the square were mostly cafés and restaurants. Their tables and chairs spilled out over the pavement in front of them.

'The Fiora, he said.'

'Over there.' I pointed to a café on the far side of the Square. 'How are we going to recognise him?'

'He'll be carrying a copy of *Playboy*.'

The Fiora was a café well frequented by Italians. Most of the customers were standing near the bar drinking small cups of expresso. None of them was displaying a copy of *Playboy*.

'We're five minutes early.' Richie pushed towards the bar. He wanted to display his Italian. '*Due capuccini, per favore.*'

'*Lo scontrino, signore.*' The barman jerked his head at the doorway.

'What's he on about?'

'You have to pay first and hand him the chittie.'

Richie, disgruntled, went to the cashier by the door, paid for two cups of coffee and brioches. The barman, smiling now, took the receipt and created two foaming cups of coffee for us.

Like everyone else we ate the brioches and drank the coffee standing up. Nectar.

I spotted the man from the Embassy the moment he came in. He was unmistakable in his fawn linen suit, spectacles and moustache, even without the magazine under his arm. That was incongruous. He did not look the *Playboy* type.

Very nonchalant and man-about-town, he went straight to the cashier, paid and took a receipt. He came to the bar quite near us and exchanged the receipt for an espresso and a glass of water. He drank the water, then picked up the tiny cup of coffee. He turned and, sipping it slowly, let his eyes run round the room till they came to rest on Richie.

Richie pushed towards him.

'Hello, Peter. Fancy seeing you.'

'Long time,' said Peter, registering Richie's glass eye and the hand with one finger missing. He drained his coffee and put the cup and saucer down on the counter. 'Feel like a stroll round the Square?'

He was nervous, not wanting to stay static in one spot. We followed him out into Piazza Navona, then formed a three-some with Richie on one side of him and me on the other.

Talking low and checking frequently that no one was close enough to overhear, Peter filled us in on the situation.

'*Colonna Nuova* issued a new communiqué this morning. There seems little doubt they're the ones who've got the General. This time they left his official NATO pass with their communiqué and a photograph of him holding yesterday's paper.'

'What sort of shape did he seem to be in?'

'Battered. He had one eye half-closed, a cut lip and a big bruise on one cheek. Their terms are the release of a hundred Red Brigades prisoners held in gaols. Of course, they know the Government could not agree to that.'

Pigeons, strutting about the Square, were moving out of the way of our feet an instant before being trodden on.

'Official British policy is that we are leaving the case to the Italians — fully confident in the efficacy of their measures and so on. There's no question of us bringing in the SAS or anything like that — '

'That's why we're here.'

'I know. That's to say Charles told me about you over the scrambler. I don't know about you officially. Mind you, the Embassy is not completely inactive. The Ambassador held a conference at Porta Pia yesterday — '

'Porta Pia?'

'The Embassy.' Peter answered my query impatiently. 'Our MI6 man there, the Military Attaché, the Consul and a few others.'

'We have an MI6 man in the Embassy?'

'Oh, yes. He's declared, of course. The Italians know all about him. He's in contact with the secret police, UCIGOS, NOCS, DIGOS and so on. The Military Attaché liaises with the *Comando Supremo Forze Armate*. All very friendly and totally unproductive.'

If there was a "declared" representative of MI6 in the Embassy, it was a fair bet that there was an undeclared one too, and his name was Peter.

We had reached the end of the Square. A Tunisian carpet-seller, weighed down with rugs and wearing a fez, approached us hopefully. Peter told him in Italian to piss off. We turned our backs on him and began to walk back towards the fountain.

'My MI6 colleague has picked up a rumour that the Brigades are working up to something really big. No, I don't mean a kidnapping. Something more like a full-scale attack on NATO installations in Italy. It would have a certain degree of

79

support from the anti-nuclear campaigners. They have a formidable arsenal of weapons in their secret dumps — even Sam Strela missiles —'

'That's not our problem,' Richie cut in, checking his watch. 'What we want to know is, has any signal been picked up from the general's kidnap alert system?'

'The kidnappers were wise to it. They took his watch off and flung it out of the car. The police found it in a ditch just outside Cassino.'

Richie chewed his lip in frustration. 'Blast! What about the ADC? Can he help us?'

'He's in an Italian hospital at Gaeta. He's out of intensive care now, I believe.'

'Anything to stop us going to see him?'

'Nothing at all. His name's Huntley-Childs. Bernard, I think. Do you want me to 'phone through and say you're coming?'

The carpet-seller was not easily discouraged. He was following behind us, keeping up a high-pitched sales monologue. The price of rugs was steadily coming down.

'Thanks,' Richie declined Peter's offer, 'but I think we'll leave it on the long finger. Could you get me the number of the NATO base at Naples? It's the signals unit I want.'

'Yes, I can do that.' Peter shot a quizzing look at Richie. 'The MA should have it. I'll ring you on that number you gave me. Did you know that Lady Stewart is arriving in Rome about now?'

'She staying at Porta Pia?'

'The Consul offered to put her up at his residence, but she said she'd prefer to stay at the Churchill Hotel. I don't think she appreciates our policy of non-intervention any more than the Italians' policy of not making any concessions to the kidnappers. HE has arranged for her to see the Pope tomorrow, and I know she's going to try to make an appeal on television. It won't have any effect. TV tears won't make *Colonna Nuova* part with such a prize captive.'

Richie said: 'Can I ask you something?'

Peter stopped to face him, his expression already blanked

out in anticipation of an awkward question. 'Does the MI6 chap at the Embassy know about us?'

Peter thought about his reply.

'Not officially,' he said. 'You should be more worried about whether his opposite number in the Russian Embassy knows about you.'

'The KGB man?'

'The top KGB man. There are dozens of them. The boss is probably quite a minor Embassy employee. The KGB have strong links with *Colonna Nuova*. They leave overt action to the Italians, but they supply them with information from their army of spies and informers. If I were in your shoes that's what I would be worrying about.'

FIVE

Johnnie was back at Palazzo Mellini when we got there. He had found a body-shop in Trastevere which would do a re-spray job on the Audi. It would be ready in five hours. Clement was in the wine store, where he had established a small armoury in a compartment walled by cases of wine. He had unpacked the Brownings and was honing the sears with an oil stone to eliminate trigger drag. Tro and Stan had come back from the Albergo Luna and were up in Franco's flat, raiding his larder. Franco himself had gone off to put it around among his contacts that a fat reward was available for information on *il generalissimo*.

Richie held a short briefing with the five of us there among the wine cases. Clement, Stan and Johnnie were to get some sleep and be ready for whatever cropped up. Tro and I were to go to Gaeta, find the ADC and see if we could pick up any leads from his account of the attack. Richie would stay in Rome to put some spunk into Franco and maintain contact with developments through Peter.

Gaeta was on the coast between Rome and Naples. We used the Autostrada del Sole for a hundred kilometres, then turned south towards the sea. The old town lay in the curved arm of a promontory. It had been a harbour since way back in Roman times. Now a warship of the United States VIth Fleet lay at anchor out in the roads. From the waterfront the houses rose steeply on a hill surmounted by an enormous fortress.

It was half an hour after midday when we drove along the harbour front. The sea was blue and sparkling. Across the bay the Aurunci Mountains were a hazy purple.

'Before we do anything else,' Tro told me, 'I've got to eat. I was feeling too bloody awful to swallow anything at the Florence *area di servizio*.'

82

We found a restaurant overlooking the harbour, ordered *tagliatelle alla carbonara* and *aqua minerale*.

'Thanks about last night.' Tro folded the menu and slapped it down on the table.

'Last night?'

'When I was sick. You were nice about it.'

'I didn't do anything.'

'That's what I mean. You didn't rush round and start holding my head or anything. You just left me to puke.'

She was not being sarcastic. We were sitting on the same side of the table, facing the room, so I could not see her expression without taking an obvious peek. So I said nothing.

'It wasn't the ham.'

'No?'

'No.'

The waiter came to put spoons, forks and a dish of grated cheese on the table. He prized the top off two bottles of Perrier and poured them into our glasses.

'Have you done jobs with Clem and Johnnie before?'

'No.'

'They both give me the creeps. Clem is so quiet and still most of the time. I mean, you'd not suspect he could erupt into such violent action. I can't make Johnnie out. He's always smiling and laughing but — '

She pursed her lips and shook her head.

'Has Richie talked to Nick since we left?'

'No,' I said. 'He couldn't get through.'

The waiter came flying back, balancing two plates piled with *pasta asciuta*. He put them before us with a flourish and smiled his benediction.

'*Buon appetito!*'

'Pat,' Tro said. 'Have we a hope of freeing the General?'

'About fifty-fifty, I'd say.'

'You know up till now only one RB hostage has been rescued. I mean, all the others have either been killed or released for ransoms. What I'm afraid of is that if Richie does find the hide-out and attacks it, they'll, you know, shoot the General. He wouldn't risk that, would he?'

My mouth was full. I took time swallowing and chewing.

'Are you wishing you hadn't come on this trip?'

My remark angered her but it took her mind off her own question.

'That's typical of a man!' she flared. 'You're just waiting for me to freak out, aren't you?'

We went Dutch on the lunch.

The hospital was in the new part of the town. The receptionist was all smiles when she heard that we had come to visit *il capitano inglese*. He was in a private room at the end of a long, gleamingly clean corridor. The ward sister, reassured by Tro's immaculate Italian, told us that they had removed two bullets and he was now much better.

'The *polizia segreta* insisted on questioning him this morning. He had hardly recovered from the anaesthetic. They made him very tired. But you are relations, no?'

'Friends.'

'Well, you can talk to him for ten minutes.'

The small room was very bare, without the flowers and cards you usually find in an invalid's room. The ADC was lying back on a fat pillow, staring listlessly out of the window. His face was not so much pale as yellowish in colour. He had lost a lot of blood. His cheeks were sunken and his eyes hollow. The bedclothes were arched by a frame over his legs to prevent the blankets from pressing on him.

'Captain Huntley-Childs?'

His head turned slowly towards me.

'Yes,' he said warily.

'Do you feel up to talking? We're trying to find out exactly what happened at Cassino, see if we pick up any leads that might help us to trace the General.'

'What are you? Intelligence?'

'We're working directly for the Cabinet Office. Official policy is to leave everything to the Italians, but we are part of an independent group that's operating separately. So it's very hush-hush.'

Only his eyes moved as Tro came from behind me round to the side of his bed. For the first time he had registered the fact that she was female.

'Not much in the way of chairs, I'm afraid.'

'It doesn't matter. We're not going to be here long. Can I ask you a few questions?'

Huntley-Childs tried to readjust his position. Immediately he gasped and winced.

'Sorry. It's my leg. It gives me gyp. The Cabinet Office, you said?'

'Yes. And we have Lady Stewart's backing — '

'Ah.' He smiled faintly. 'Lovely person. She's coming down to see me. She 'phoned from Rome this morning. If Lady S knows about you then you're okay with me.'

'Would you tell us what happened?'

The ADC ran his tongue over pallid dry lips.

'The General had been inspecting a NATO base near Naples — at Bagnolo, actually. You know he's D SACEUR. He wanted — on his way back to Rome — to pay a visit to the war cemetery at Cassino. A private visit. He fought there in 1944. His brother was in the same regiment and was killed the day the Monastery was captured.'

'You said a private visit. So no one knew he was going there?'

'Well, as a matter of courtesy, we notified the Mayor of Cassino. But the General didn't want any fuss or ceremony.'

Rather than stand staring down at the sick man, Tro crossed to the window and looked out at the US warship.

I asked: 'What time did you get there?'

'Eighteen hundred hours. There were very few people about. The Mayor had provided a couple of police and they had already cleared the cemetery. The General wanted to be alone so when he entered the cemetery I asked the guards to keep at a reas — ' His face twisted again. The talking was an effort. His colour had become even worse. ' — a reasonable distance.'

Instead of asking a question I tried to guess the answer. 'These were Italian guards, members of GIS probably?'

He nodded. 'Yes. In a car behind. Four of them. Good chaps. Armed to the teeth.'

He reached a hand weakly towards the bedside table. A glass of water had been put there by the nurse. I handed it to him and he drank.

'I stayed pretty close to the General as he walked across the cemetery. I always do when he's out and about. But you can't . . . You can't crowd somebody when they're at their brother's grave.'

He looked up at me. There was an appeal in his eyes. He was blaming himself for not guarding the General more closely. I took the glass from his hand and put it on the table again.

'He was — standing in front of the grave. I was about ten yards away. Suddenly — there was this long burst of machine-gun fire from beyond the perimeter fence. The Italian guards went down. I don't know whether they were hit or taking cover. Somebody had lobbed smoke grenades behind us, men had come through the hedge and were running towards us, firing from the hip, they got me with a burst and I went down, then — '

The rush of words checked. The ADC pressed his lips tight together and closed his eyes. He was too weak to resist emotion and did not want to give way to tears.

'The General saw me go down — and — he charged them.' The ADC struggled with his breathing. 'He went for them with a roar, waving his blackthorn — he charged them — '

Huntley-Childs was unable to go on. The ward sister came hurrying in. She glared at me accusingly.

'— *ha parlatto abbastanza.*'

I took the hint and nodded to Tro. The sister was soothing the ADC's brow. As we reached the door I heard him say something.

'He — '

I went half-way back across the room.

'He went for them to stop them — firing at me. They didn't want to kill him — so they jabbed him.'

'Jabbed him?'

'Yes. With a syringe. Just before I — passed out.'

'Can I ask you one last thing? What was his brother's name

and regiment?'

'Wilfred Stewart. Greenshire Yeomanry.'

'*Signore*,' the sister implored me. '*Per l'amor di Dio —* '

Cassino was twenty-five miles inland from Gaeta. The road wound through the Aurunci Mountains. As we drew nearer we could see the huge Benedictine Monastery standing on its sheer hill nearly two thousand feet above the plain. We crossed the autostrada and entered the town.

I stopped so that Tro could ask an old man the way to the military cemetery.

'*Il cimitero militare?*' His face cracked in a smile. 'But there are so many — the Italian, the Polish, the French, the German, the British — '

'It's the British we want.'

The British War Cemetery lay out on the open plain to the south of the town. We left the car in the nearby *parcheggio* and walked back to the entrance. St John's Wort grew in tumbling abundance on the banks flanking it. Inside, the trees planted by the War Graves Commission had grown in thirty-eight years to maturity. Italian students had brought their books and were sitting reading on the shaded lawns. It might have been a public park — except for the rows upon rows of bone-white headstones lined up in orderly squadrons. Acres of them. In front of each was a miniature bed of brilliant flowers, carefully tended by the Italian gardeners. There was not a weed in sight.

From high above, the windows of the rebuilt Monastery gazed down upon the silenced army.

'Jesus Christ!'

Tro's whisper was scarcely audible. I went to the hut where the names of the dead are recorded, found the entry for Wilfred Stewart and the code giving the location of his burial place.

Tro had not moved. Not speaking, we walked between the echelons, heading for the furthest corner. The grave we were looking for was tenth from the end in the thirteenth row of its block.

Captain Wilfred Stewart
The Greenshire Yeomanry
Aged 21 years
Killed in action 18 May 1944
'Dust as we are the immortal spirit grows
Like harmony in music'

'He must have been standing just here. They came through that fence over there.'

I started towards the gap I could see in the wire mesh.

'Coming, Tro?'

She was still standing reading the inscription. When she heard me she came out of her reverie and followed me.

There were still some ejected sub-machine gun shells in the grass by the hedge. The wire fence had been cut with shears. On the other side was a stony track bordering a field. Forty feet away a *contadino* was hoeing along a row of vegetables.

'I wonder if he saw anything.'

'He wouldn't be alive if he had.'

'There's just a chance, Tro. See if you can chat him up. He's more likely to talk to you.'

The *contadino* stopped working to watch us approach. He was suspicious and nervous.

'*Ciao*,' Tro said with a smile. '*Buona sera*.'

He answered gruffly in a dialect which I could hardly understand. Tro made sense of it. The best I could do was follow the gist of the conversation.

'We English. Friends of the abducted *Generalissimo*.'

'Not police?'

'No. This is the son of the *Generalissimo*.'

The *contadino* gave me an awed look and crossed himself.

Yes, he had been here. Taking a rest in the shade of the hedge. Two cars had come up the track. He had kept out of sight because he did not like the look of the men who got out of them. Later, when he heard the shooting, he lay doggo, so he didn't see much.

How many men?

Six. They had radios with aerials on them in their hands as well as guns. They all tied masks over their faces.

88

What make were the cars?

One was an Alfa-Romeo. White. That was the one they put the *Generalissimo* in.

Had he seen the registration number?

FI. It was from Firenze. He had not noticed the number.

Did he hear their voices?

No. He was down there by the hedge, keeping out of sight. He knew he was dead if they saw him. We wouldn't tell the police he'd seen it, would we?

Tro reassured him that we would not give him away.

I said: 'He's done very well. It's not much but it's a lead. We must give him some money.'

'Don't give him money. A packet of cigarettes will do.'

The *contadino* at first made a show of refusing the packet I had in my pocket, but in the end he accepted it, embarrassingly grateful. It earned us one final tit-bit.

'*Shera un gran barbudo calvo.*'

'What did he say?'

'There was a big chap with a beard and a bald head.'

Both the Italian gardeners were watching us as we walked back to the cart.

'That was a good idea - son of the *Generalissimo*.'

'Yes,' Tro agreed. 'He'd never have told the police what he told us. These peasants don't trust the *carabinieri* and they're shit-scared of reprisals from the terrorists.'

'Someone in the Commune at Cassino must have tipped them off. I don't think there's much chance of *us* finding out about that.'

I would like to have contacted Richie to tell him that we had a lead — a slender one but a lead all the same. But I did not trust the telephone and the CB was too open, even if I could make contact.

We drove back through the town and took the road leading to the autostrada junction. It was roughly the same time of day as the kidnapping.

I parked the Saab on the side of the road leading to the *peaggio* post on the autostrada. The blue-uniformed employee was already wagging an admonitory finger at us as we approached his glass-fronted kiosk.

'*Vietato.*' He pointed to the Saab. '*Vietato parcheggio li.*'

Tro explained that we were Brits, trying to pick up the trail of the kidnappers of *Il Generalissimo.*

'English police?'

'No. Not police.'

'Intelligence Service?'

Tro made a non-commital gesture. 'Something like that. Were you by any chance on duty two evenings ago?'

We were in luck. He had been. But he had seen nothing. The *mobile* and the PS had already questioned him.

He broke off to hand a ticket to a driver entering the motorway.

Tro said: 'Do you remember a white Lancia with a Firenze registration?'

'I don't take much notice of the cars. There is not time.'

To illustrate the point he broke off again to hand out another ticket. The cars were coming more frequently now and the rest of our conversation was punctuated in this way.

'You might have noticed this one,' I said, guessing how it must have been. 'The car was crowded, three or four young men and a bundle in the back. One of them was bald and had a beard.'

'A bundle in the back?' The attendant's memory was stirring. 'A white Lancia, you said?'

'Yes. Firenze registration.'

A British car had come from the direction of Cassino, with an elderly couple in the front seats. The woman had trouble getting her window lowered. Obligingly the attendant went round to the driver's side and handed him a ticket.

'There *was* a fellow with a funny accent,' he said, as he regained his kiosk. 'I remember him now.'

'Florentine?'

'Perhaps. He asked me how far it was to Naples, though. That's south.'

'How far south is the next exit?'

'Venafro. Nine kilometres.'

90

It was worth a try. The enquiry about Naples might have been a blind to conceal the fact that they were going north. We went back to the car, bought a ticket from our attendant friend and drove onto the south-bound carriageway of the Autostrada.

We came upon it three miles later — a white Lancia, Firenze registration. It had been thoroughly pillaged. The wheels had been taken off and every removable fitting stolen.

It is almost impossible to stop in Italy without seeing someone in a field not far away. This time it was an oldish woman assembling a bundle of brushwood for a bread oven. She'd be from the small farmstead shaded by cypresses half a mile away.

Tro went across to have a word with her. I stayed to examine the Lancia, hoping to find some vestige of the General. There was nothing.

Standing in the road I could see Tro talking to the woman. A small boy had appeared from nowhere. The conversation was accompanied by vigorous gestures and pointing towards Venafro. Then Tro came walking back to me.

'The small boy saw them,' she reported. 'He hasn't told anybody because he stole the radio from the car. He's a sharp one. They transferred a sick person to a big Mercedes-Benz which was waiting here.'

'Did he see the registration?'

'Yes. Not the number, but it had a Bologna prefix.'

It was very much in our favour that Italian cars carry a registration number with two letters which indicate the town of origin.

'That's two from the north. They were stolen cars, of course, and they'll certainly dump the Mercedes as well.'

We drove the remaining couple of miles to the Venafro exit. The attendant there was no good to us. He had been off duty two days ago. We crossed the autostrada and re-entered it on the north-bound carriageway. It was easy to imagine the kidnappers doing exactly the same thing.

Half way back to Rome Tro suddenly came out of a day-dream.

'Dust as we are the immortal spirit grows — how did it finish?'

'Like harmony in music.'

Back in Franco's flat we walked into a full-scale row between Richie and Johnnie. Richie had found out that Johnnie had picked up an Italian girl in the Corso Vittorio Emmanuele and taken her back to the Albergo Luna to keep him company during his siesta.

'I can't sleep properly unless I've got a woman in my bed,' he was saying.

'You might have talked in your sleep, blown the whole bloody show.'

'I don't talk in my sleep,' Johnnie retorted, still defiant. 'And I don't snore either.'

'That's immaterial. Are you so stupid you don't realise that *all* our lives depend on the tightest security — '

'Stupid? Did you call me stupid?' Johnnie's voice had gone unpleasantly quiet. There was no trace of that jocular smile now.

Tro chose that moment to put her oar in.

'I suppose you had to pay her,' she said sarcastically. 'What did she charge you?'

Johnnie turned on her in fury.

'Yes, I did pay her. She was a tart. But at least she was honest about it. She wasn't one of those bitches who waggle their arse at you and then scream rape if you lay a hand on them — '

'Are you saying that I — '

'*Cool it*!' Richie shouted. 'Has anybody seen Franco? He's been gone for six hours now. I'm getting worried about him.'

Clement and Stan had kept well clear of the row. They'd had five or six hours sleep and you could see the difference. They both shook their heads.

'He won't 'phone,' Richie said. 'He refuses to believe me when I tell him there are no taps on his line. Now, Pat. How did you get on with the ADC?'

Johnnie, muttering, went out to resume his watch over the

cars and depot. Coming in we had seen the Audi in its gleaming coat of new black paint. It bore a different set of number plates, still British and with a Z registration. Probably from the car of some luckless tourist who'd fallen victim to the Rome car-thieving Mafia.

I gave Richie an account of our visit to the hospital at Gaeta and the enquiries we'd made at Cassino.

'It's a lead,' he agreed grudgingly, 'but I'm not sure those Florence and Bologna registrations mean much.'

'Did you contact the signals unit at Bagnolo?'

'Yes. They've got two vehicles quartering the whole of central Italy. One of them is concentrating on the Rome area. According to Peter, SID believe the General is somewhere in the Rome area. That's the *Servizio Informazione Difesa*, their equivalent of Military Intelligence.'

'Wouldn't it be worth suggesting that they switch one vehicle to the Florence-Bologna area?' I suggested. Richie was not reacting as I'd hoped to the lead we had provided.

'I might do that if they haven't come up with anything by tomorrow,' he conceded. 'Lady Stewart's broadcast may produce something. She's speaking at nine o'clock this evening. *Radio Televisione Italiana* have taken it up in a big way. Nothing the Italians like better than real live sob-stuff. It should be a proper tear-jerker.'

'For Christ's sake, Richie,' Tro protested.

'They've laid on special lines and answerphones to handle the flood of calls they're expecting, and the Prefect of Police has allocated a detective to sift through them. I'd like to have one of my own men on that too. You've got the best Italian of any of us, Tro.'

Tro nodded resignedly. 'You want me to do the baby-sitting, right? I guessed that was how I'd wind up.'

At eight o'clock five of us were sitting round Franco's television set — Richie, Clement, Johnnie, me and Tro. Stan was down in the courtyard keeping an eye on the cars and store, monitoring the people coming in through the main gateway. He had one of the hand-held CB sets and another was switched on in the flat.

Richie had been to the bank with Clement as bodyguard. He had withdrawn two hundred million lire in cash. It was bulky enough to fill a suitcase. Since the episode on the road from Geneva, he was more than ever conscious of the risks involved in sitting on such a large sum of money.

Lady Stewart's appeal was prefaced by an exceedingly emotional introduction by the commentator. She herself was the embodiment of dignity. In fact, I wondered whether her British reserve and control would fail to make an impact on the Italians; they might think that she was callous and unfeeling. She spoke very slowly and distinctly, pausing so that the translator, also female, could keep pace with her. She appealed directly to every woman listening. She invited them to consider how she and her family felt. She begged them to help find her husband and bring about his release. The most effective part was at the end when she asked them to inform her personally. She gave them a special number they could use to get through to her at her hotel. She finished with a little sentence of Italian she had learned.

'*Donne d'Italia, una moglie inglese vi implora: Aiutatemi a ritrovar il mio marito.*'

'Fantastic!' Tro said, as Richie switched the set off. 'What a super person!'

'How do you think the Italians will react to that?'

'The women will love it. I mean, she's just what they expect an English milady to be like. Those lines are going to be busy.'

Richie's rule was that none of us were to move about alone. It fell to me to take Tro over to Lady Stewart's hotel near the Villa Borghese in the now less conspicuous Audi.

She had just got back from the television studios and was in her upstairs suite. She received us in her bedroom. She was wearing the same clothes as when I had seen her in London. I even wondered if she had been to bed since then. The lines of stress and fatigue had deepened but her manners were impeccable. She still showed that amazing consideration for other people.

The sitting-room of the suite had been turned into a miniature communications centre. The Prefect of Police's detective was in there with an employee from the telephone service. All incoming calls were being taken on the telephone answering systems so that they could be recorded and analysed.

'How kind of you to come, my dear.' She had sized Tro up in a flash and had shown not a flicker of surprise or disapproval at her unisex attire. 'But I am afraid you are not going to get much sleep. The calls are already coming in.'

'I shan't mind, Lady Stewart. I mean, that's what I'm here for.'

I could see that Tro had been smitten from the start by the older woman's charm. She was gazing up into her face. 'We saw your broadcast. It was super.'

'Thank you. I felt I was a little wooden, but the last thing I wanted was to make a spectacle of myself on television.'

'No, you were marvellous.'

A little embarrassed by this adulation, Lady Stewart turned to me.

'Mr Malone. You have had no luck so far. Otherwise you would not be here.'

I told her that we had seen Huntley-Childs and paid a visit to the Cassino cemetery.

'Ah, yes. Dick always goes there when he visits Naples. He and his brother were very close. I never knew Wilfred, of course. I'm afraid I'll have to postpone my visit to Bernard. Did Mr Bryer tell you that the Pope has consented to see me tomorrow? I am going to try and persuade him to make a broadcast appeal also.' Her eyes had taken on that inward-looking expression. 'We have not much time.'

'What makes you say that?'

'I can feel things more strongly here in Italy. Dick is near to cracking, I know it.'

I said, in spite of myself: 'Do you have any feelings about — where he is?'

'He's not far away. I feel him close. And it is still dark.' Her voice sank. 'Very dark.'

95

Tro's mouth had dropped open in astonishment. From beyond the curtains and the double-glazed windows came the muted chatter of the traffic in the Via XX Settembre.

The door from the sitting-room opened. The girl from the telephone service put her head through.

'Milady. There has come a call we think is interesting. You wish to come and listen it?'

'Yes. I will come.' Lady Stewart turned back to Tro. 'You are staying here, my dear? I did not quite catch your name —'

'People call me Tro. But my real name is Katrina.'

I arrived back at the flat hard on the heels of Franco. Johnnie had relieved Stan on gate duty. Richie and Clement were in the sitting-room with Franco. It was obvious from the atmosphere that there had been an important development.

'Come in, Pat,' Richie said, a little impatient at the interruption. 'Franco's had a nibble. He's just been telling us.'

Franco took his spectacles off and began to polish them. Without the glasses his eyes were vague, the flesh around them pallid and scored by wrinkles. When he put them on he looked like an intelligent human again.

'I must have been in twenty bars today.' His voice was hoarse from talking incessantly in smokey cafés. 'One has to lay one's lines out and then wait for the fish to come to the bait. And this evening I had a most promising bite.'

'Yes, yes, Franco.' Richie had heard this bit before. 'You said he was interested in the reward. Have you arranged to meet him?'

'*He* made the arrangement. Either I accept or I ignore it.' Franco shrugged and spread his hands. 'I am to meet him in the Capella San Nicolo at the Vatican tomorrow at ten o'clock. Alone, of course.'

'What about money?'

'I said we would pay an advance of ten million lire. A hundred million to follow if the information leads us to the General.'

*

96

Before joining the others in the Palazzo for breakfast, I went down to the Corso and bought some papers from a newsstand. Richie had spent the night in Franco's flat in case anything came through on the 'phone. As Clement and Johnnie had been able to sleep during the day they'd shared the night watch — as well as taking turns in one of the rooms at the Albergo Luna. I'd shared the other with Stan, and discovered that he snored. The *Corriere della Sera* had the Chamonix story on the foreign news page.

The police of Haute Savoie had found four corpses in two cars at the bottom of a gorge beside Route Nationale 205. All had been shot by a bullet from the same pistol. The killings, the police spokesman said, had all the characteristics of a gangland execution. As all the dead were guest-workers from Calabria it could well be a Mafia execution.

The situation on the Polish frontier was tense. According to one newspaper American reinforcements had been airlifted across the Atlantic to reinforce Central Army Group in Germany. Three British batallions in Northern Ireland had been switched to Northern Army Group. There were rumours that a Polish artillery commander had ordered his guns to fire on Russian tanks which had infiltrated across the frontier. Europe was a tinderbox waiting for the spark that would ignite the conflagration.

'Looks as if we may have got away with it,' was Richie's comment when he read the Chamonix story. His good eye toured the four of us sitting round the table. Stan was down in the courtyard doing his spell on watch. 'No one must mention that incident again. Not now or ever.'

The telephone rang at half-past seven. Franco knocked his chair over backwards as he went out to the hall to answer it.

'He's shit-scared,' Johnnie said in a low voice. 'I hope he's not going to freak out on us.'

Franco was back almost at once.

'It's Tro,' he told Richie. 'She wants to speak to you.'

Richie listened for a long time, making a few notes on the message pad.

'Right, Tro,' he said at last. 'I think it's best if you stay there. Can you get some sleep? . . . Okay.'

He put the receiver down and came back to us.

'They recorded over two hundred messages during the night. People were ringing from all over Italy. Mostly women. A lot of them were simply messages of sympathy and good wishes. The usual crop of abusive or obscene calls. In amongst it all were a few giving information which might be relevant. These are being analysed by the police, but Tro's made a note of a couple that might be worth following up if Franco's informant turns out to be a dud.'

'Where are they? Up north?'

'Pescara and Civitavecchia. We'll keep them on ice till we've done this Vatican lark.'

Franco was becoming more and more nervous as the time approached for us to leave. Richie, Clement, Johnnie and I would be behind him, but that was a good deal less than comprehensive insurance. He would have to do the last bit on his own. A knife or a bullet could perfectly well be waiting for him in the Capella San Nicolo.

Clement, uncommunicative as ever, had gone down to the wine store to check the trigger responses of the Brownings yet again. Richie fitted Franco out with one of the bullet-resistant waistcoats. Apart from the fact that it clashed violently with his suit, it looked like an ordinary waistcoat. The hundred 100,000 lire notes were packed inside a thick guide to the Vatican. The pages had been cut to form a concealed compartment when the book was closed.

Richie made him stand in the light of the window to be inspected, with the book under his arm. He was too dapper for a tourist. With the ill-fitting waistcoat, his crinkly hair and those large glinting spectacles he had more the appearance of some clerk to the Curia. He was clutching the book tightly to conceal the trembling of his hands.

'Have I time to ring Cecile?'

'God! What a time to want to telephone your wife.'

'The condemned man's last request,' Johnnie commented, laughing.

'Go on, then,' Richie told him. 'Be careful what you say,

though.'

Franco consulted his watch. 'She'll still be in bed.'

'Alone, I hope.'

Franco gave Johnnie an injured look. He went out to the hall and began to dial. After a delay we heard him murmuring endearments to his English wife.

He left the flat at a quarter past nine. Alone. It was possible that he would be picked up by a tail somewhere between the palazzo and the Vatican. Johnnie, Clement, and I left at intervals during the next quarter of an hour. Richie would come last, leaving poor old Stan as usual to keep watch.

I could not see any of the others as I walked through the narrow streets and emerged on the bank of the Tiber opposite Castel Sant' Angelo. It was going to be a glorious day. The sun was already warm.

Under the bridge the waters of the river were a muddy grey. Up on the battlements of the Castel I could see a row of tiny heads peering down at the sheer drop, picturing the body of Puccini's Tosca plummetting down after her suicide leap. The stream of people in the Via della Conciliazione were all moving towards St Peter's. On the other side and a little ahead of me I picked out the squat figure of Johnnie, ambling along with his bow-legged walk. He had bought himself a straw hat, hoping it would make him look more like a tourist.

The grey wooden crush-barriers that kept the crowds under control were still positioned in St Peter's Square. The vast area now seemed empty under the gaze of the Twelve Apostles on the roof below the dome. Only at the northern side was there a crowd round the caravan that housed the Vatican post office. The faithful were queuing up to despatch letters to all parts of the world bearing Città del Vaticano stamps and postmarks.

I turned right out of the Square and walked slowly round the outer walls of the Vatican towards the tourist entrance at the southern end. I allowed the hurrying posses of trippers to flow past me. Franco would pass through the turnstiles at ten precisely. We would follow at one minute intervals.

At three minutes past the hour I walked up the spiral ramp

that led to the turnstiles, paid my money and went in.

The visitor to the Vatican has a choice of four routes, each offering different features. Franco would be following the Green Route. It included the Chapel of St Nicholas. We had a lot of walking to do before we reached it.

The marble-floored galleries that led through the Vatican Museums to St Peter's itself were echoing to the languages of five continents. Through the windows, across the gardens, I could see the famous dome, rising majestic above the trees. I had picked up the black curly head of Franco a little in front of me. He was dallying as if reluctant to make the rendezvous. Richie and Clement were not far behind me, masked by a group of Spanish children escorted by nuns. I could not see Johnnie. He was too short to stand out in a crowd.

Studiously ignoring each other, we let ourselves be carried by the current down the narrow steps into the Sistine Chapel. The place was more like a market square than a church. The incongrous sound of a telephone shrilling pierced the cackle of the mob. People almost fell over backwards trying to look at the paintings on the ceiling. We stood dutifully, gazing at the Last Judgement on the end wall, waiting for Franco to move on.

It was ten to eleven when he entered the Stanze di Rafaello. The Chapel of St Nicholas lay beyond the furthest of the rooms decorated by the Renaissance artist. Franco appeared to be fascinated by one of the frescoes in the last room. He stood staring over the head of a small nun at the Apparition of the Cross. But he was not seeing it. He was trembling visibly.

By now Richie, Clement, Johnnie and I were all in the same room. We were each of us staring at different pictures. The hands of my watch had moved round to four minutes to eleven.

The Chapel of St Nicholas is at the end of a suite of rooms. There's no exit beyond it. A lot of visitors miss it out altogether. So it happened that, apart from the little nun, we five were for the moment alone.

For some minutes I had been aware of a babble of strong male voices coming closer. Now a group of about a dozen young Italians came bursting into the room we were in. They were a tough bunch, perhaps a football team on a visit to Rome. They seemed totally out of place in the Vatican.

The little nun cast them an apprehensive glance and hurried towards the small door in the corner that led to the Chapel of St Nicholas. If she had hoped to find sanctuary there she was soon disabused. The young Italians spotted the pointing arrow and crowded in after her, laughing and joking.

It was a minute to eleven. Franco was staring at the door of the Chapel. He made no move to follow them. Instead, he suddenly turned round and walked towards me. His face was the colour of ash.

He thrust the book at me and muttered: '*Non posso più.*' My mouth was open as I watched him walk rapidly out of the room, back the way we had come. I could see his point. Occupied by the twelve thugs the Chapel of St Nicholas did not seem all that attractive.

I caught Richie's eye. He looked at his watch and jerked his head at the Chapel. His meaning was obvious. 'Get in there.'

'Sod you,' I mouthed at him.

As I walked towards the Chapel I could hear the babble of voices from inside. The sound was very similar to a pride of hungry lions demanding meat. Holding the book close against my chest I walked in.

The Chapel was tiny. The twelve large Italians almost filled it. I could smell their body odour and the garlic on their breath. I was outnumbered twelve to one. There were enough of them to tear me apart and eat me. No one would ever know. I pushed in amongst them. They jostled and rubbed against me. At any moment I expected the guide book to be snatched from my hands as a stiletto slid under my ribs.

The sweat was beginning to start out on my own body when I realised that I was being borne back towards the doorway. They were moving out, pushing and shoving towards the narrow gap. I had to fight against the stream to avoid being carried with them.

Suddenly they had gone. I was alone in the Chapel under the starry blue vault. But not quite alone. The little nun was kneeling in front of the tiny altar, her hands joined. She was deep in prayer.

Where was the contact? It was a minute past eleven. I stood there, surrounded by the delicious frescoes of Beato Angelico. The expulsion and stoning of St Stephen seemed less horrific when portrayed in brilliant hues and crimsons offset by gold leaf.

The little nun finished her prayers and rose to her feet. She turned towards me and for the first time I looked into her face. It was wet with perspiration. She'd been as frightened as me.

'*Voi siete Franco?*'

The voice was a man's!

'No,' I answered in Italian. 'He couldn't come.'

Greedy, scared eyes peered out at me from under the cowl. The mouth was working nervously. Those pink cheeks had been recently shaved. I could see a fresh cut on his chin.

'You have the money?'

'Yes. Have you the address?'

The fake nun produced a folded sheet of paper from under his habit. He handed it towards me, but would not relinquish his hold. I opened the book to show the notes neatly packed inside.

'There's a million lire here.'

'And the rest?'

'You'll get it if we find the *Generalissimo*.'

'You must not delay. They are going to move him tonight.'

'Okay. How do we contact you?'

'I will telephone.'

He seized the book, at the same time relinquishing the slip of paper. I unfolded it quickly and saw one line of writing:

37 Vicolo Sant' Agnese in Agone.

As I refolded it and put it in my pocket he was already hurrying out through the door. I could hear the voices of another party about to enter the Chapel. I collided with them in the entrance. They glared at me with resentment as I pushed past.

The little nun had disappeared. Richie, Clement and Johnnie were staring anxiously towards me. From the room beyond, a party of Germans were flooding in. They were being dragooned by a masterful woman with cropped blonde hair. Their faces were dazed by a surfeit of culture. I reached Richie's side just before they engulfed us.

'Didn't he come?' he hissed at me.

'It was the nun.'

'Christ!'

SIX

You can't hurry out of the Vatican. By eleven in the morning the corridors are crammed by a long snake of people moving as slowly as porridge through a constipated gut. It was nearly half past before I at last broke out into the sunshine of the Viale Vaticano. The moisture of sweat was cold against the small of my back. I went into the café across the road and had a long, cold beer.

I saw Richie, Clement and Johnnie emerge, alone and at intervals, from the Vatican entrance across the road. We had agreed to make our way back to the Palazzo separately, as we had come. It was possible that the contact had accomplices who would try and tail us after the exchange had been made. As far as I could see no one was following the others and I was reasonably sure that no one was tailing me. It seemed that the little nun was acting alone.

There was a newspaper kiosk a little way down the street. I bought a *Pianta-Guida di Roma* and looked up the Vicola Sant' Agnese in Agone. It was a small street not far from the Pantheon. In that area all the streets are narrow. By making quite a small detour I could go back to the Palazzo that way.

The centre of Rome is really quite a small area. It is often quicker to get around on foot. In a car you can waste a lot of time unless you know the one-way streets.

Ten minutes walking brought me to the little square at the end of the Vicolo. There was a café with half a dozen tables under striped umbrellas set out on the cobbles. On the corner was the regulation Virgin in her niche.

I walked slowly up Vicolo Sant' Agnese, checking the numbers. It was a deep canyon, where the sun's rays only penetrated for a brief period in the middle of the day. There was little movement of traffic. The sound of voices and footsteps echoed between the walls. High up, outlined against the sky, was a fringe of green. Owners of the topmost flats with access to the roof had created gardens up there. There were plants at street level too, in window-boxes or pots just standing on the ground. One plant had seeded itself in a hole in the wall. An anonymous hand had rigged a string to encourage it to grow upwards.

A paper dart thrown from above planed past my ear before making a three-point landing in a puddle of water. I looked up and saw a young girl at a window smiling down at me. Could anything clandestine happen in these surroundings, where everyone must know what their neighbours were doing?

I passed two antique shops, a toy shop, a dress shop with a tiny window packed with brilliant garments — all of them small premises. From the wall a stone cherub smiled at me. Above it a brash sign proclaimed the local headquarters of the Partita Communista Italiana. Some of the inhabitants had brought chairs out onto the pavement so that they could sit and gossip. As I came abreast of number 37 I saw that it was the shop of a piano restorer.

I stopped outside the window, loitering as if my interest had been caught by the tabby cat sitting just inside the glass. Beyond, I could see seven or eight pianos. Most of them were awaiting repair. There was one baby grand which had been beautifully restored and might be for sale. A man in a grey apron was just picking up a cloth to resume polishing it. He glanced up, gave me a quick inspection and decided that I was just another window-gazer. Two more cats, one black and one Siamese, stared at me from the tops of their respective pianos, daring me to come in. There was a door at the back of the shop leading to a darker region beyond. It was about thirty feet from me.

The premises at number 35, to the left of the piano shop, were empty. A blind had been pulled down behind the dirty window. On the wall was a house agent's notice: *Si Vende.*

Reflected in the window I could see an old man looking out at me from his window across the street. I walked straight on and headed back towards the Palazzo without going along Vicolo Sant' Agnese again.

Everyone had returned to the flat except Franco. They were drinking coffee laced with whisky in the sitting-room. Richie was warning Johnnie not to rib the Italian for chickening out.

'Anyone's nerve can fail. I don't want him to lose too much face. Hello, old Pat. We thought we'd lost you, too.'

I handed him the slip of paper the little nun had given me.

'37 Vicolo Sant' Agnese in Agone. It's only ten minutes walk away from here. I came back that way and had a look at it.'

'Ten minutes from here? God, that's a laugh. We've been assing around for more than a day and he's within a mile of us all the time.'

'I'm not so sure. I came back that way and had a look at it.'

I told Richie about the piano shop and the empty shop beside it which could conceivably be large enough to contain a "people's prison".

'Doesn't sound very probable,' Richie said dubiously. 'All this may have been just a trick to relieve us of ten million lire. We've got to check it out, though.'

'The nun said they were going to move him tonight.'

'Tonight! Then we can't hang around. It's going to be impossible to do any clandestine surveillance. We'll just have to push a couple of bods in there and be prepared to escalate if we hit opposition. What do you think, Clem?'

Clement, leaning against the door jamb, shrugged. 'Your operation.'

'Why not just give the information to the Italian police and let them suss the place out?' Stan suggested.

Richie threw him a baleful look.

'We haven't come all this way just to hand the whole thing to the Italians on a plate. Besides, they'd probably cock it up.'

It would have been completely out of character for Richie to opt out of "the job" at this stage. The more the action escalated the happier he would be. And if there was anything he personally could do to ginger things up, he'd do it. His craving for danger and excitement made him a hazardous man to work with, but never a dull one.

Franco's key grated in the lock. Richie shot us a warning glance. When he came in the Italian looked ghastly. He had gone through a bad time at the Vatican and now he was tormenting himself with remorse. To judge by the aroma on his breath he had been stiffening himself with something stronger than Irish coffee.

'I am sorry,' he said. He avoided looking at Johnnie and Clement. 'I just . . . I guess you think I'm a coward.'

'Forget it,' Richie told him. 'It worked out all right.'

'I'll make it up to you.' Franco took his glasses off and began to de-mist them.

'Of course you will. Could you start by going over to the Churchill and bringing Tro back here? I'm going to need my whole squad for this job.'

Franco cheered up at being given a job to do. He took the keys of his own car and went straight out again. Johnnie was despatched to borrow a couple of four-door saloons from the streets of Rome. Clem and Stan went down to the store to look out the Brownings and a few stun grenades. I drew a map for Richie and filled him in with every detail of the area around the piano repair shop.

By the time Franco came back with Tro forty minutes later Richie had his plan ready. Johnnie had procured an Opel and a Ford. As the ignition keys were still in the pockets of their owners, they would have to be started by joining two wires together. That did not matter, as we would abandon them within an hour or two.

Tro was remarkably fresh. The flow of messages had eased during the morning and Lady Stewart had been able to cope with the situation. She had insisted on Tro taking a few hours sleep in her bedroom.

'She's a fabulous person!' Tro was starry-eyed about the General's wife. 'I mean, she's in the thick of this terrible crisis and she can still think about other people. You know, I don't believe she's slept a wink since her husband was kidnapped. They make you feel, you know, *humble*, people like that.'

She shook her head in amazement. Richie winked at me. Clem and Johnnie were expressionless.

Richie held a short briefing in the wine store. Everyone memorised the layout of streets round the piano shop and the map I had drawn of the immediate area. There were enough Brownings for Richie to issue one to everyone except Franco and Tro. Clem and Johnnie had a couple of stun grenades each. They carried them in their jacket pockets, where they bulged like large cakes of soap. Richie had a length of the Cortex explosive and a couple of detonators.

'Don't barge into me,' Johnnie warned Franco as we moved out to the cars. 'These things are primed already to detonate on impact. They're liable to go off if you give them a bang.'

In the courtyard Johnnie opened the bonnet of the stolen Opel. Using a spare length of wire he connected the terminal on the coil to the non-earth terminal on the battery. He pressed the direct contact switch on the starter motor and the engine fired. He closed the bonnet and then gave the Ford the same treatment.

I noticed a certain relief on Tro's face when she realised that she was not going to ride in the same car as Clement and Johnnie. She climbed into the back of the Ford with Richie. Stan took the wheel. I sat in the front passenger seat. Franco was driving the Opel with Johnnie beside him and Clement in the back. In a two-car convoy we drove out of the Palazzo and down to the Corso.

Five minutes later our two vehicles nosed through the little square and entered the Vicolo Sant' Agnese. Stan drove past the shop and stopped ten yards beyond it, just before the lateral alley. From his window opposite Number 37 the old man was still staring out. Richie, Tro and I dismounted.

Franco had stopped fifty yards further back. Clement and Johnnie had already got out. The two cars effectively sealed off a section of the street from other vehicles. A third car had already stopped behind Franco. The driver was blowing his horn furiously. He stuck his head out of the window and started shouting. Franco went into his act, giving back as good as he got. He jumped out of his car. We could see him waving his hands. He was giving a convincing demonstration of the

Italian whose driving credentials and parentage have been questioned and who is prepared to argue the point at operatic volume.

People in the street were already hurrying to join in the fun.

Richie took up his position outside the door of the shop. I opened it for Tro, politely standing back to let her in first. The tabby cat had moved from the window to a shelf on the wall. The Siamese and the black cat had not stirred. There was no welcome for us in their stare.

The piano-restorer had heard the door open. He came out from the room at the back, chewing and swallowing.

'*Buona sera, signore — signorina*. What can I do for you?'

We had come well forward into the shop.

'I am looking for a good secondhand piano. Are any of these for sale?'

The shopkeeper was nervous. He ran an apprehensive eye over Tro. She was obviously something new in his experience.

'Yes, *signorina*. You wish an upright or a grand?'

Tro laid her hand on the beautifully restored baby grand. 'This one — it is for sale?'

'*Si, signorina*. That is a very good piano. One of our best makers.'

'How much?'

The man glanced towards the door. Richie's broad back had moved into view again. He pondered for a moment.

'Two million lire, *signorina*. But perhaps for you — '

'Could I try it?'

The restorer made an apologetic gesture.

'It has not yet been tuned, signorina. *Magari* — '

The shop door was opened abruptly. Clement and Johnnie bustled in. Outside, Richie moved into the shop front to prevent anyone else entering. The two newcomers were already drawing their Brownings. Ignoring the shopkeeper they walked rapidly towards the door at the back.

'*Scusi, signori* — ' Alarmed, the man in the grey apron tried to stand in Clement's way. Clement bundled him aside. I

109

grabbed him.

'*Ma, cosa succede? Cosa vogliono?*'

'*Stia fermo,*' I told him.

He was not dangerous. I could feel him trembling in my hands. Clement, covered by Johnnie, had disappeared into the dark area beyond the door. Johnnie followed. I heard a crash as of a door being kicked open. I waited for shots, explosions.

A minute passed, perhaps two. The piano restorer was gibbering with terror. Then Clement appeared in the doorway.

'Place is empty. But something has been happening here. Call Richie.'

Clement covered the shaking man. I went to the door to call Richie. Down the street Franco was putting on a tremendous show. An admiring crowd had collected. No-one was paying any attention to the sudden influx of customers into the piano shop.

I reversed the sign hanging on the glazed door so that the CLOSED side showed outwards.

In the back room a naked bulb hung from the ceiling. It illuminated a parlour about twenty feet by twelve. On the side towards the empty shop next door there was a gap in the wall. Bricks had been removed to make a rough doorway.

'Come in here,' Johnnie called from beyond the jagged hole.

Richie and I stooped to go through. We were in the back room of the adjoining shop. It was a kitchen-cum-sitting-room. A door opened into a crude lavatory with a dirty washbasin. A flight of stairs coiled up to the floors above. There were signs of recent occupation, probably several people. The floor was covered with cigarette ends. The smoke in the air was still fresh — the acrid smell of Italian tobacco flavoured with cannabis. Dirty plates, mugs and glasses had been left on the tables, chairs, even the floor.

'Look at this.'

Johnnie had opened the door of a large cupboard at one side of the room. He shone his torch inside.

'You've checked upstairs?'

'Yes.'

I went over with Richie to look into the cupboard. Immediately the bad smell hit me.

The cupboard was just big enough to contain an iron bedstead and leave two feet clear beside it. There was no window. On the bed was a hair mattress. The stuffing was bursting out of it. Under it stood a slop pail, which had not been emptied. That was where the smell came from. Lengths of flex dangled from the corners of the iron bedstead. Someone had lain there, tied by the wrists and ankles. On the floor were animal droppings. They were too big for mice. Rats, more probably.

This was a people's prison.

Richie took Johnnie's torch, played it over the bed. On the mattress was a patch of dried blood.

'That must have been from the cut on his cheek.' The roving beam of the torch focussed on the wall near the far side of the bedhead. 'See that?'

Scratched on the dirty surface, probably with a finger-nail, were three recognisable initials: MRS.

'He left his signature.'

'There's something else underneath. Can you read it?'

I peered more closely while Richie kept the beam of the torch fixed on the letters. There were two words. I read them out.

'Pian. Piano.'

'Doesn't make sense.' Richie snapped the torch off. 'It's time we were getting out of here.'

We backed out of the cupboard. I shut the door to keep the smell in. Richie and I followed Johnnie through the gap in the wall.

'I'm going to talk to that shopkeeper,' Johnnie growled. He raised his voice. 'Bring him in here, Clem.'

'Make it short,' Richie warned. He went off to see how Franco was holding out.

Clement dragged the shopkeeper into his back room and sat him down on an upright chair. Johnnie stood close in front of him. Tro came to the door and stood watching. She was scared by what might be going to happen, but fascinated in spite of herself.

The man was already blathering his innocence. He was not part of the gang, he protested. They had come two days ago and forced him into it. This had all happened because of his ne'er-do-well son. He'd kept bad company ever since he was a child. And now Mamma was in hospital, dying . . .

Johnnie took his left hand and bent the middle finger back. The Italian shrieked.

'Gag him, Clem.'

Clement found a polishing cloth, tied a knot in the middle. He forced the knot between the man's teeth, fastened it behind his neck.

Johnnie said, in his Neapolitan Italian: 'I am going to give you one more chance and then I intend to break every finger in your hand. Understand?'

The man tried to rise. Johnnie pushed him down again. Somethng soft rubbed against the back of my leg. I jerked it clear. Looking down I saw the Siamese cat. It was purring, staring up at me, beseeching affection.

'We know the *Generalissimo* was here. What we want you to tell us is where they have taken him.'

Crack.

The sound of the joint breaking was surprisingly loud. The middle finger lolled back loosely. The man squirmed under Clement's hands.

'Take the gag out, Clem. No screams, mind.'

When the gag came out, Johnnie's victim was whimpering with pain. The tears were rolling down his cheeks.

'They did not tell me. They broke the wall and took him in the next house. I swear to you I know nothing — aach!'

Clement clapped a hand over his mouth. Johnnie, still holding the hand, had rotated the loose finger.

'If you scream you get another joint broken. Now, cut out the crap and tell us, *where have they taken the Generalissimo?* Okay, Clem.'

'By the blood of our sacred Saviour, *signore,* I only know

112

that they took him away this morning — hidden in a piano. I do not know where. Kill me, *signore*, but do not destroy my hands. Without them I cannot live. What will become of Mamma?'

'Put the gag in again, Clem.'

Behind me Tro said in a low voice: 'You're prepared to stand for this?'

'He's telling the truth, Johnnie,' I said. 'He doesn't know any more.'

Richie's shout came from the outer door of the shop. 'Everybody out! The police have arrived.'

'We can't just leave this cretin.' Johnnie glared down at the cowering Italian. The man had seen a death sentence in his eyes. An even greater terror convulsed his features. No smiles and wrinkles on the ex-mercenary's face now. 'That piano wire will do.'

He took a step towards the workbench where a metre length of new wire lay.

'You haven't time,' Clement said. 'Let's move.'

Johnnie hesitated then pushed his nose to within an inch of the piano restorer's face.

'You say a word about this — *one word* — and I'll come back and break your nine remaining fingers.'

'Not a word, *signore*. I swear it.'

As we followed Tro towards the street I saw the Siamese cat jump onto its master's lap. The tabby and the black had not moved from their posts.

We had been in the shop less than five minutes. Back along the street the string of cars held up by Franco stretched back into the little square. I could see the blue of a police car behind them, its roof light flashing. Two uniformed officers were pushing their way through the vociferous crowd.

Franco was walking unhurriedly towards us, trying to look as if the fracas had nothing to do with him.

'Into the Ford everyone,' Richie directed crisply.

Tro tried to take off in a run. I grabbed her arm, forced her to walk at normal pace like the rest of us. Stan was sitting stolidly in the driving seat, ignoring the questions of the old man who had hobbled out of his house in a desire to be helpful. Richie, Clement and Johnnie piled into the back seat. I slid into the front one and hauled Tro onto my knee. Richie was holding the rear door open for Franco. Shouts came from the direction of the crowds as people realised that the principal actor had walked off stage. Franco sprinted the last twenty yards. The car was already moving when Richie pulled him in. He fell across the knees of the three in the back.

'Hey!' Johnnie shouted. 'Mind those grenades.'

'Oh, God!' I felt Tro's body shiver.

'Left here,' I told Stan. 'It takes you back to the Corso.'

We were all flung sideways as Stan rounded the tight corner. The rear wing clouted the wall under yet another statue in a niche. Tro anchored her bottom more firmly in my lap.

'What a shambles,' Clement observed.

'Drive across the river,' Richie told Stan. 'We'll dump the car in Trastevere.'

'Okay, mate. If you'll tell me the way.'

'It's just as well they weren't there. The whole thing went off at half cock. The General would have been dead before we got to him.'

'Okay, Clem,' Richie said. 'Point made. So we learned a lesson or two. We'll do better next time.'

We had abandoned the Ford near the Church of Santa Maria in Trastevere and made our way back to the Palazzo in pairs. Now the seven of us were in the wine store, standing around or sitting on cartons of Chianti, Lambrusco or Lacrima Cristi.

'The shopkeeper must have known where they were taking him,' Johnnie went on. 'I was just persuading him to talk when Pat goes soft.'

'He didn't know any more than he told us,' I said, for the second time. 'Why did the General write his initials and those two words? Pian, Piano.'

'Obviously he heard them talking,' Johnnie said, 'and realised they were going to take him away in a piano.'

'Pian, Piano?' Tro repeated. 'That's the Italian equivalent

of — let's think. Softly softly. But, I mean, why would he write that?'

'I think Johnnie's right,' Richie said. 'He overheard them talking.'

'But the little nun's tip was a good one. We know that now. He said he'd 'phone about collecting the reward, that right, Pat?'

'Some time this evening.'

'Okay. Franco, I want you to stay near the 'phone till he calls. When he does, pretend to be very pleased. Say we're ready to pay the balance. Try to fix a meeting with him. You don't have to go yourself. One of us will do it.'

'No, no,' Franco said quickly. 'Please. I know I flaked out in the Vatican this morning, but it will not happen again. I promise you.'

Franco wasn't looking at Johnnie and Clement but he must have been aware that they were contemplating him sceptically. He desperately wanted to prove himself in their eyes.

'Fair enough,' Richie decided. 'Try and fix a rendezvous where we can give you good back-up. You can hand him the money, no problem about that. Then we'll tail him and see where he leads us.'

Tro was impatient to rejoin Lady Stewart. It was likely that the volume of incoming calls would increase in the evening. I drove her round to the Churchill Hotel and escorted her up to the suite.

There were signs that the tension was beginning to get to the older woman. The usually firm mouth had started to sag. There were deeper lines of fatigue round her eyes. But her inbred courtesy never failed. She would not let me go till I'd had a drink.

'The Consul brought me these.' She picked up a bottle of Noilly Prat and a bottle of Gordon's gin and took them to the drinks table between the windows. 'When he asked me if there was anything I wanted I said that what I needed most of all was a stiff gin and French.'

She poured three parts of gin and one of vermouth into a mixer, added ice and stirred clockwise. 'Dick taught me how to mix a Dry Martini. He always insisted on it being done properly.' She stirred the mixture again, this time anti-clockwise. She poured out three glasses and handed one to Tro and me.

I noted that Tro, who was scornful of what she called snob drinks, was prepared to accept a cocktail from Lady Stewart.

I said: 'Tro told me you had a good response to your broadcast.'

The two women exchanged a smile. Tro was hanging on every word the General's wife said.

'The response was amazing. Some of the messages were very moving. But really the flood was too much. It will take a long time to sort through. But it has been a great help to me, you know. The Italians are a very warm-hearted people. Ordinary Italians, not the — '

Her eyes were glistening. I did not try to fill the short silence. Any comment would have sounded trite. The curtains had been drawn back and the noise of traffic in the street below was louder, more urgent than the night before.

'His Holiness was very kind, very sympathetic. A wonderful man. It was a most moving experience meeting him, even though I am not a very devout Catholic. But he did not feel he could speak for me on television. He confided to me that he is considering making an appeal to the world for peace in this present crisis and he does not want to blunt the impact. Of course, I can see that one man's life is not important when we may all be facing annihilation. The Ambassador told me the situation is very serious.'

One man's survival did indeed seem insignificant in the context of nuclear holocaust. But history showed that the fate of nations could turn on the life or death of a single man.

'He gave me his blessing.' Lady Stewart stared out through the window unseeingly and half smiled. 'That is not a trifle — a pontifical blessing.' She turned to Tro. 'You don't believe in that sort of thing, do you, my dear?'

'I'm not sure what I believe, Lady Stewart. What was that

116

writing on the stone at Cassino, Patrick? Something about dust.'

Lady Stewart guessed what she was talking about and supplied the answer. ' "Dust as we are the immortal spirit grows like harmony in music." Wordsworth. It's from *The Prelude*.'

I finished my cocktail and put the glass down. We had decided not to tell Lady Stewart about our abortive raid. It would only distress her. I could not resist the temptation to put her extra-sensory perception to the test.

'You said yesterday that you felt your husband quite close. Do you still have that feeling?'

Her eyes swung round to study me thoughtfully. She had guessed the reason for my question but did not resent it. Tro was glaring at me for setting what she saw as a trap.

'Yes. I did feel that yesterday. Very strongly. But it's funny. All day I have had a feeling that he was moving away from me — further and further.'

It was an effort to hold her eyes. They were not really focussed on me. At least, not on the surface of me. Nor were they gazing through and past me. I had an odd conviction that they were probing into an infinity that was inside me.

Daylight was fading when I returned to Palazzo Mellini. Richie, Franco and Stan were sitting round the low coffee table in the sitting-room. A map was spread out between them.

'You've been a time, old Pat,' Richie chided me.

'Lady S was in a talkative mood.'

'Well, we've got work to do. Franco's contact 'phoned about a quarter of an hour ago. Franco has to meet him at the Column of Nero in the Roman Forum at one a.m.'

I saw then that the map was a plan of the Foro Romano, the centre of Ancient Rome. Its excavation had been one of the better monuments to the regime of Mussolini.

'It closes at dusk but there are several ways of getting in. The little nun has chosen a good spot. There will be no one about and visibility will be low. The moon won't be up and as

117

the Forum is below modern ground level it's in a pool of darkness. You still want to go through with this, Franco?'

'Yes, yes. Of course,' Franco spoke with a vehemence that was intended to impress himself as much as anyone else. He had his spectacles off again and was polishing them. 'Franco is not a chicken. I will show you.'

The Foro Romano was a quarter of an hour's walk away. Richie and I had been along there to look at the spot the little nun had chosen for the rendezvous. We'd decided to leave the cars behind as an unnecessary encumbrance. They were also an additional means of police identification. Franco left the Palazzo at midnight, an hour before the rendezvous time, accompanied by Richie and me. He was now wearing one of the bullet-resistant jerkins. It gave him more protection than the vest. He was carrying a suitcase with a billion lire in it, in notes of one hundred thousand.

Clement and Johnnie followed separately. A recent shower of rain gave Johnnie an excuse to wear a mackintosh borrowed from Franco. Under it he was carrying one of the Armalites. With the skeletal stock folded back it was only thirty inches long. An image-intensifying telescopic sight was in the Florentine leather gentleman's handbag slung over his shoulder. Clement was the expert with a hand-gun; Johnnie's special skill was the sniper's rifle.

We went by narrow side-streets, passing again through the Piazza Navona. The lights blazing from the cafés were reflected from the wet paving stones. We could see the last of the customers inside the restaurants, lingering over their dinner. Voices and laughter floated out.

From the Piazza we cut past the Pantheon, then down into Piazza Venezia. Ahead of us the huge wedding cake of the Monumento Vittorio Emmanuele gleamed in the diffused light of the street lamps. Crossing the street was a major hazard. Cars were careering round very fast from the Via dei Fori Imperiali.

Clement and Johnnie had got there more quickly and were already waiting at the eastern corner of the monument. There were few pedestrians about. At the far end of the Via the floodlit Coliseum showed up stark against the overcast sky. Between us and it was the ancient classical site, well below the level of modern Rome. Here and there ruined columns and arches loomed up from the pool of darkness. The floodlights beamed on them made the surrounding shadows deeper. To the right rose the Palatine Hill with its illuminated brick walls.

Richie led the way up a broad flight of steps that led to the Campodoglio. From here Franco could climb over the rails and down into the Forum. A little higher up, some twenty yards from the stairway, an outcrop jutted over the enclosed area. It would give Johnnie a view of the Column of Nero. The range was about two hundred yards.

'All right, Franco?'

Franco nodded and ran his tongue over his lips. He was visibly trembling, holding tight onto his suitcase.

'Clem will go with you as far as that archway.' Richie pointed to a well-preserved arch about a hundred yards from the perimeter. 'Johnnie will be covering you from up here. With that Armalite he can hit an egg at two hundred yards. If the little nun tries anything he'll drop him.'

'It is as dark as a cow's belly down there.'

'Don't worry. He can see you clear as daylight.'

Johnnie went up to the outcrop to position himself. He had fifteen minutes to find a position, fix his sight, adjust his range and focus on the Column of Nero.

Clement scaled the perimeter fence. A pair of image-intensifying goggles dangled from his neck. Franco handed the suitcase over to him. Then Richie and I helped Franco across. We heard them slithering carefully down the slope below.

'Someone coming,' Richie murmured.

We leaned our elbows on the rails and turned our backs. A girl and her boy-friend were walking up the steps, clasping each other tight under a shared raincoat. They went past laughing, too engrossed to spare any attention to a couple of mad tourists staring down at the area where the Roman

119

Senators had strutted two thousand years ago.

When they had passed we moved up to a look-out point close to Johnnie. He was lying on a patch of grass in a marksman's position, his legs splayed out in a V shape. His left elbow had found a hole in the ground and his right hand cradled the perforated shield of the Armalite's barrel. The night scope was already fitted. He was peering through it with one eye closed. Richie and I lay down a few yards away.

'Okay, Johnnie. You can see the target?'

'Lovely. How are we for time?'

'Five minutes to go.'

Richie took the image-intensifying goggles out of the shoulder satchel he was carrying. He handed them to me.

'You'd better have these. Two eyes are better than one.'

I put the harness over my head and focussed the protruding eye pieces. Staring down into what to the naked eye had been impenetrable darkness, I could see a luminous green world devoid of shadows. Even the small stones on the ground were visible.

It took me a moment to find Clement and Franco. They were about half way from the perimeter to the column. Clement had put on the night goggles, a twin set of my pair. The eye pieces protruded like the eye-stalks of some enormous jungle insect. I swung the goggles towards my right and upwards. Johnnie appeared startlingly close and clear. He had taken up an aiming position, his cheek snuggling the Armalite. He shifted his position slightly, then lowered the rifle and waited.

Focussing again on Clement and Franco I saw that they had reached the Arch of Septimus Severus. Clement patted Franco on the shoulder and rested his gun hand on a ledge to cover him for the thirty yards that separated him from the column. I saw Franco look upwards. He was trying to pick out the tip of the column against the luminous under-belly of the clouds. With the glasses on it was hard to believe that down there it was pitch dark.

I began to search the area for any sign of the little nun. Nothing was moving except Franco.

All over Rome the bells in their clock towers started to chime, each one claiming that it was hitting the hour on the nail. Franco had reached the column, groping for the stone with his free hand. The other still clutched the suitcase.

The base of the column was square, surrounded by two levels of steps. Richie had warned him to stay on this side of it, never to let himself be lured round the corner out of our view. He stood with his back to the stone on which Nero's exploits were recorded indelibly in stone. He peered into the shadows round him. Even now he did not put the suitcase down. In my goggles the bullet-proof jerkin under his jacket reflected an eerie luminosity. I took a quick look at Johnnie. He had brought the Armalite up into the aiming position.

When I focussed on the area round the column again I saw something move. Suddenly the little nun was in my sights. He had come out from behind a fallen block twenty yards from the column.

'He's there,' I hissed. 'Have you got him, Johnnie?'

'Got him.'

The little nun was still wearing the religious habit. He had hitched the long skirt up round his hips to give himself freer movement. Carefully, putting each foot forward with caution, he made his way towards the column. Though they were clearly visible to me, neither man had yet seen the other. Franco was not aware of the little nun till he came up onto the steps beside him. I saw Franco start.

Clement was holding the Browning with the familiar two-handed grip. I knew he had the little nun covered.

'They're together now,' I whispered to Richie. 'Franco's talking to him. Now he's handing the case over.'

Both the men down there were very frightened. You could see it in their movements. They kept darting glances into the darkness. The little nun put the case down on the step. A light flashed briefly and was quickly shaded by a hand. He was crouching down, opening the case to check that the money was there.

The double snap as the fastenings sprang back was a sharp sound, etched clearly against the rumble of the city. Then, from up on the Palatine Hill, there came a much louder crack. I saw Franco reel back as if he had been punched violently in the chest. The thud of the bullet striking was like a sledge-hammer blow.

Franco had sprawled back against the column. At that moment he was a ragged shape in my goggles outlined against the stone. Abruptly the shape changed. The head had dissolved. An instant later the second crack from the Palatine Hill reached my ears.

The little nun had involuntarily straightened up. At once he was punched forward onto his face and the third report reverberated from the hill.

'Jesus God!' Johnnie exclaimed out loud

Richie said: 'What's happened?'

'Franco's been shot. So has the little nun.'

'What's Clem doing?'

'He's waiting. He's gone to ground behind his stone.'

'Johnnie, keep him covered. Those shots came from up on the hill there. I saw the flashes.'

So someone else had a rifle with a night-scope up on the Palatine Hill. The three reports had not disturbed the night life of Rome, though they could have been audible to the few people walking along the Via.

'Clem's starting to come back,' I told Richie.

'Damn! Johnnie, stay where you are and keep me covered. I'm going down there.'

'For God's sake, *why*? Let the money go.'

'It's not only the money. I don't want Franco identified.'

'That sniper is still up there.'

'Maybe not. He got his men. Why should he hang around?'

'I'll come with you. Down there is no place for a one-eyed guy.'

We met Clement at the place where he and Franco had climbed over. He was just about to come back over the top. Richie told him what he intended to do.

'Blast! Should have thought of that.'

We did not need to ask him to give us additional cover as we made our sortie to the Column of Nero. As I guided Richie across the broken ground and round the vestiges of ruined buildings it was some comfort to know that we had a marksman of Clement's calibre behind us.

Five minutes had passed since the shooting. The deadly marksman could still be on the Palatine Hill, watching and waiting.

The thirty seconds Richie and I were on the steps of the column could have been measured by the thumping of my heart beating at double speed. It was merciful that the night goggles did not give a full colour picture. The bullet had smashed away half of Franco's head. His brains were splattered against the carved stone. Even in monochrome green he was a terrible sight.

Richie and I moved as fast as conjurors. We were very much aware that we were sitting targets, clearly visible to anyone with a night-scope on the hill above. I closed the suitcase and picked it up. Richie reached into Franco's breast pocket for his wallet and identity papers. He quickly felt in his other pockets and removed anything he found there.

Still no shot came.

Richie crammed the contents of Franco's pockets into his own. I started to leg it away from the column, then remembered that Richie could not see in the dark. Grabbing his sleeve with one hand and the suitcase with the other I ran him back to where Clement was standing with his automatic at the ready.

We were climbing the perimeter when shouts drew our attention to the entrance to the Forum on the Via. A couple of police cars had drawn up at the kerb, their roof lights flashing. Someone had heard those three shots coming from the Palatine Hill.

SEVEN

The ringing of the telephone woke me. I came to, conscious mainly of the crick in my neck. Gradually I realised that I was lying on the sofa in Franco's sitting-room. Across the room Richie had pulled two chairs together to form some sort of couch. Clement and Johnnie had dossed down in the bedroom.

The four of us had demolished a bottle of brandy after getting back from the Forum. We needed something to relax the tension, shock and grief we felt at what had happened. The lead that had been so promising had turned into a live wire in our hands.

Richie had insisted on us all staying under one roof. There had been a leak somewhere about the rendezvous in the Foro Romano. Someone knew that the little nun was selling information. The burning question was, did they also know who the purchasers were?

Stan had not joined the drinking session. His police training had given him a more sober and responsible attitude. He knew that someone had to remain clear-headed. And besides, he did not have any reason to blame himself for Franco's death. We did. Stan had kept watch all night down in the courtyard.

I staggered to my feet. The brandy was knocking my skull and I'd only had three hours' sleep. As I picked the 'phone up I was certain that the call came from the police. The bodies of the little nun and Franco must have been found hours ago.

'*Pronto. Chi parla?*'

'Patrick, your voice is funny. What's happened?'

Tro.

I cleared the phlegm from my throat. 'Tro, something dreadful has happened.'

'You sound as if you'd swallowed a plateful of winter grit.

124

Listen, Lady S has had some very interesting — '

Befuddled as I was, I remembered to check the dials of the bug-alert which Richie had attached to Franco's 'phone. The needles were jerking.

'Tro,' I said loudly. 'Hold it. This line's very bad. You read me?'

'I can hear you all right.'

'The line is bad, not clean. Can you get back here? We need you. The — ah. Someone's gone for a Burton.'

'What are you talking about?'

'He's being measured for a golden crown and a harp — '

'*God*!'

'You read me?'

'Yes. I'll come right away. Who is it?'

'Take a taxi. Okay?'

'Yes. Okay. I'll be — '

With a gulp she rang off.

I woke Richie. He snapped immediately into full wakefulness. Like the rest of us he had flopped down without taking his clothes off.

I told him that the bug-alert was giving a positive reading. He went to confirm it for himself, putting a call through to the reception clerk at the Excelsior Hotel.

'It's bugged all right. Could be a routine police bugging. They're doing a lot of that since the General was kidnapped. I wonder if Franco checked the bug-alert when he took the call from the little nun.'

When Tro arrived she found us in the kitchen drinking large cups of strong coffee. We had cleared our heads with Prairie Oysters mixed from Franco's well-stocked drinks cupboard. Johnnie and Clement were in the bathroom, shaving and jolting themselves into wakefulness with cold baths.

I told Tro what had happened. She sat down, shocked.

'You shouldn't have let him,' she reproached Richie. 'He only did it to prove himself to you.'

'He insisted. What did you expect me to do? Would you rather it had been Patrick?'

Tro's head jerked towards me. Her eyes were very wide. I wondered what was going on in Richie's mind to make him pick my name out of the hat.

Tro gave a small shiver. 'Who killed him?'

'Obviously someone found out that the little nun was selling information. Maybe they killed Franco as well to discourage the purchasers. It was effective because we have no idea who did it. That lead has gone completely dead — perhaps that's an unfortunate way of putting it.'

Tro pulled a chair up to the kitchen table and sat down. The little knot on top of her head was working loose. Strands of hair poked out in different directions.

'I've got a new lead for you. We had a call late last night. Lady S was sure it was genuine. She had, I mean, one of her feelings about it.'

'That's nothing to — '

Tro held up her hand to block Richie's interruption. 'Wait a minute. Don't be so quick to scoff. There's a, you know, a sort of coincidence.'

'All right.' Richie was smiling sceptically. 'Go on. Tell me.'

'The detective and the telephone person had pushed off about midnight. The flow of calls had eased off. Lady S was getting some sleep. About time too! Anyway, I took the call from this woman. She sounded — you know, very frightened. Wanted to talk fast and ring off. But she insisted on talking to Lady S personally — '

'This wasn't on the tape?'

'I'd stopped using the answerphone but the call was taped. I mean, they all are.'

'Did she speak in English?'

'Let me tell you, for God's sake!'

'Sorry.' Richie poured himself a third cup of black coffee.

From the bathroom came Johnnie's shout and gasp as he lowered his body into a cold bath.

'She spoke in English. That may have been because she was nervous about someone, you know, overhearing her. Very bad English. I think I'll have some coffee, okay?'

126

I got up to fetch an extra cup.

'Anyway, I woke Lady S up and she took the call. She got very sort of excited about it. I mean, she was like lit-up. She was sure this was the genuine thing.'

Richie's smile broadened.

'Okay, laugh. But wait till you hear this. Thanks, Patrick.' She smiled at me and poured coffee into the cup I'd brought. She added three heaped spoonfuls of sugar. 'I listened to the tape afterwards. The woman's message was very disjointed. She claimed she knew where the Generalissimo is being held. She kept repeating the name. Pian di Capretto.'

'Where's that?'

'Somewhere north of Florence. But don't you see? *Pian, piano.*'

'The General's message?'

'Right! He may have heard them talking about, you know, where they were going to take him.'

In the bathroom Johnnie, towelling himself, had started to sing. He had a very strong tenor voice and was giving a rendering of *Ridi, pagliaccio.*

I said: 'That ties in with the lead we picked up at Cassino. The cars they used there were from Florence and Bologna.'

'Pian di Capretto,' Richie repeated. 'Does that sound like the name of a town?'

Tro was holding the cup in two hands with her elbows on the table.

'Pian comes in quite a lot of place names. Usually villages. It means like a flat shelf on the side of a mountain.'

Richie shook his head. 'Sounds improbable to me. Their safe houses are usually in cities where goings and comings and strange faces are not conspicuous.'

'They may have changed that tactic,' I cut in, siding with Tro. 'In fact, their town hide-outs have not worked out so well. Dozier's prison was located and but for a bit of bad luck we'd have blown the Rome people's prison yesterday.'

I glanced round to find Tro looking at me. She had a far-away expression as if she was not really listening to what I was saying. As our eyes met she dropped hers.

'Well, let's look it up on the map, anyway.'

I went down to the courtyard to fetch the set of Touring Club Italiano maps Stan had bought in London. It took us a little time to find Capretto. It was a small village to the west of the Bologna-Firenze autostrada, about mid-way between the two cities.

In the end Richie agreed that Tro and I should follow up the tip. He would not release Stan, Clement or Johnnie to come with us. The killing of Franco had shaken even Richie and the knowledge that there was a bug on our telephone suggested that our flimsy cover had been blown. There had not been time to search Franco's pockets thoroughly. The forensic experts would eventually find some clue to his identity, even minus head. I was certain that the KGB had informants in the police department that could bring unwelcome visitors to the flat. From now on there would always be a guard of two at Palazzo Mellini.

Tro's suggestion that we could make the trip quicker in the Audi was turned down.

'You can take a hire-car,' Richie told her. 'That'll be less conspicuous. You and Patrick can pass yourselves off as tourists.' He added with a grin: 'Pretend you're a honeymoon couple.'

Tro withered him with a glare of fury.

We had been motoring for miles along a minor road that followed a river meandering between steep hills. Abruptly we rounded a corner and there ahead of us was the vast arch of the autostrada spanning the valley. At either end the mouth of a dark tunnel yawned where the highway burrowed under the mountain. The lorries, buses and cars shuttling busily to and fro a thousand feet over our heads looked as small as toys.

Down here in the valley we were a hundred years away. The motorist who speeds from Bologna to Florence on the modern highway sees only glimpses of this wild and mountainous region.

With Tro at the wheel of the hired Alfa Guilietta we had reached Florence before the shops closed at midday. I'd made two essential purchases — a pair of powerful binoculars and a set of the 1:50,000 maps issued by the *Istituto Geografico Militare.*

Tro had relished the drive over the Futa Pass. The turning for Capretto was a few kilometres beyond the top. From there the road plunged down to follow one of those deep valleys that lead into the remote regions of the Appenines.

Capretto was the only village served by this road. It nestled in a crook of the hills, the last section of the road climbing to it in a series of steep hairpin bends. Beyond it the mountains formed as it were one half of a bowl, their peaks rising to seven thousand feet.

'You know Capretto means kid, like a young goat,' Tro explained. 'Like you have to be some sort of goat to get up there.'

Not many strange cars came to Capretto and the few that did were not very welcome. A narrow cobbled street with houses close on either side led into a small piazza with the usual fountain in the middle. One side of the square was open, offering a superb view back down the valley. The arch of the autostrada viaduct was visible in the distance. The people stared at us suspiciously as we got out of the car, their faces closed and expressionless. This was a community sealed off from the world, and it wanted to stay that way.

A few Martini umbrellas outside quite an up-to-date café provided a splash of modernity. We strolled over. The proprietor was a young man with the manner of a city dweller. His was the first welcoming face we had seen.

I ordered two espressos. He showed surprise that I could speak Italian. He squeezed a couple of deliciously strong coffees from his Gaggia and automatically supplied a glass of water with each.

I looked out into the sunlit square. Someone from here had telephoned Lady S. They might well have used the telephone on the wall at the end of the bar.

We drank our coffee Italian style standing at the bar. The proprietor seemed inclined to talk. Not many tourists came up here, he told us. We were German? Ah, English!

129

A couple more locals drifted in casually, pretending not to notice us. They had obviously come to satisfy their curiosity. Their eyes flicked covertly towards Tro as they ordered their beers.

I groped in my mind for the history of World War Two. 'There was fighting up here during the war, wasn't there?'

'Yes. There were many partisans.' The proprietor added with a hint of defiance: 'The Germans were defeated before the Allies arrived.'

In a generation history can change.

'My uncle was in this part of the world,' I said, untruthfully. 'He used to talk about a place called Pian di Capretto.'

'Pian di Capretto?' The name was obviously familiar to him but he repeated it as if he was hearing it for the first time.

'Yes. Isn't it near here?'

'Yes. Further up. But the road is impassible now. The winter floods caused an avalanche and it was completely blocked.'

'There's nobody up there anyway,' one of the locals said, showing a row of brown teeth with two gaps in it. 'That fellow spent a lot of money but he's not got much joy of it.'

'Oh?'

'There was a mine up there years ago,' the café proprietor explained. 'It's been out of use since before the war. A rich industrialist from Bologna bought it up and built himself a chalet. But he can say goodbye to his money, as Vittorio says. They'll never repair that road.'

The industrialist had evidently not made himself popular in Capretto. Everyone appeared to be pleased that he had lost his money.

Tro was keeping quiet, pretending she could not understand the conversation. As she shifted her position the locals stared with open frankness at the movement of her hips in their tight jeans. A third and older man came in and ordered a glass of Vin Santo.

The conversation ambled on. I learned that Pian di Capretto was five miles and a thousand feet further up. No car

130

had been there since the previous summer.

'You can see the old mine from the hill over there,' the proprietor said, as I paid for the coffee. 'If you feel like a walk, that is.'

I took the binoculars and the 1:50,000 map of the area from the Alfa. The track to the hill led through a farm where hens cackled and a tethered dog barked. Beyond that the track worsened and the climb became steeper. An old man had come out of the farmhouse. He watched us all the way to the top of the hill. We were sweating before we reached it.

The view from the summit of the knoll was awesome. Below lay the village of Capretto. To our left the winding road by which we had come snaked away across the floor of the valley to the viaduct. To our right a narrow road more like a track led uphill from the village round a flank of the mountain. It climbed towards a vast semi-spherical bowl formed by the high mountains behind. A mile or two from the village it took a loop round a dip in the hills and plunged straight into a vast landslide which completely obliterated it over a length of two hundred yards. Beyond that the track snaked on, climbing more and more steeply in tight hairpins till it reached a green shelf high up against the grey rocky slope of the mountain. There it ended. Indeed, the terrain beyond was so precipitous that no vehicle could have penetrated it. Three peaks dominated the range. My map told me they were Monte Vergine, Monte Calvo and Monte Magro.

Through the binoculars I could see a few old buildings with fallen-in roofs. Beside them stood a brand new single-storey chalet. The steep Swiss-style roof had a wide overhang. The doors and windows were shuttered with stout battens.

'The place is deserted,' I said in disgust. 'So much for Lady S's perceptions. We've come two hundred and fifty miles for nothing.'

'Can I, please?'

Tro grabbed the binoculars before I could replace them in their case. She put them to her eyes and adjusted the focus.

'Make a back for me, will you?'

I turned my back on her. She rested the binoculars on my right shoulder, standing on tip-toe behind me.

'Marvellous setting! That house must have a fabulous view. But I wouldn't like to live in it. There's something, you know, frightening about those mountains. They're like ready to fall on it.'

'Come on,' I said. 'Let's get back to the car.'

'Wait a minute! I think I've seen something! Can you lean forward a little?'

She focussed the glasses more carefully. I could feel her warm body pressed against my back.

'Is that an aerial? At the right-hand end of the house?'

I took the glasses, refocussed them. She had sharp vision. I could just make out a vertical hairline, black against the grey rocks behind. As I watched it sank out of sight.

'There *is* someone up there. They put up an aerial and retracted it.'

'I *knew* this was the place!' Tro was exultant. 'I had a feeling about it too.'

I lowered the binoculars. If it was them, how had they got there? With a hostage, too. There was no route in from the back. That was clear from the map.

'If we could only find the woman who made the 'phone call — '

I shook my head. 'We have already aroused too much interest. If that's a hide-out they must have watchers down in Capretto. The thing now is to slip away as unobtrusively as we can. Perhaps we could work on that honeymoon couple image a bit more?'

When we reached the village Tro entered into the spirit of my suggestion. She pressed herself against me, walking as if we were in a three-legged race with our inside knees tied together. We each put our arms round the other's waist. When she let her hand slide down I did the same. I could feel the thrust of her right buttock against my fingers at every step she took.

As we crossed the little piazza a young man got up from the wall bordering it. He had been sitting close to the hired

Alfa. He strolled towards us with studied casualness, exuding bonhomie. I'd seen his type before. They are usually pimps.

'You are interested in seeing Pian di Capretto?'

'Yes,' I said, relinquishing my hold of Tro. 'An uncle of mine fought in these parts during the war.'

'Ah, you are American?'

'No. English.'

'This was an American sector,' the young man reproved me. 'Americans and partisans. The English were to the east of the Futa.'

'That's right,' I said smoothly. He had turned to walk beside us to the car. 'He was a liaison officer with the American Forces.'

'And the *signorina*. She is English too?'

'Yes.'

'You speak very good Italian for an Englishman, *signore*.'

The compliment was spurious. I was sure he did not belong to Capretto. He was more the city type.

'I studied Italian at school.'

'And now you are touring Italy, no? Looking for places off the beaten track.'

'That's right.'

'It is not possible to go to Pian di Capretto any more,' he assured me vehemently. 'No-one has been up there since last summer.'

'So I gather. But I've seen all I need. I just wanted to get the the general picture.'

Tro had made no attempt to conceal her distaste for the importunate Italian. She climbed into the car and started the engine.

He looked at the number plate with the RO registration. 'You have come from Rome today?'

This was turning into a bare-faced interrogation.

'No. Florence.' I opened the passenger door of the car. 'We have to be in Bologna this evening. *Arrivederci*.'

'*Arrivederci, signore*.' He bowed to Tro. '*Signorina*.'

I got into the passenger seat and slammed the door on him.

133

'Too bloody nosey by half,' I muttered.

She drove towards the exit from the square, leaving him staring after us with a faintly mocking smile.

'Look over there,' I said. 'The woman outside the grocer's.'

I had seen a woman in a neat black widow's outfit watching us with a particularly intent expression. She gave me the impression that she would have liked to come and talk to us but did not dare to do so. We had to pass quite close to her as we left the piazza to go back down the narrow main street. She held my eyes with hers as we drove past.

We were half-way down the steep hairpin section below Capretto when I happened to glance backwards towards the town.

'There's a car behind us. It's coming pretty fast. Looks like a Maserati.'

Tro glanced round, saw that I was not strapped in. 'Fasten your seat belt.'

I pulled the buckle round and snapped it home.

Just in time. Instead of braking Tro had dropped a gear and was accelerating towards the next corner. It was a right-hand hairpin. She put her inside wheels off the tarmac surface onto the loose gravel at the edge of the road. The Alfa bounced and lost adhesion, the back end broke away. Tro kept the power on, using throttle to force it round the corner. I was flung against the seat belt as the car rocked. She had flicked it broadside in order to approach the next bend crabwise. We rushed towards it with the nose pointing towards the scenery on the outside of the corner. At the last minute she over-corrected the slide, apparently attempting to ram the bank on the inside. Again, power not steering took us round.

We careered down that hill in a series of power slides. The car was always sideways, never pointing down the road ahead. Tro's arms were constantly whirling the steering wheel. Every few seconds her hand dropped to the gear lever to make a change. Her feet danced on the pedals like an organist's as she balanced braking against acceleration.

Somehow, against all known laws of centrifugal force, she kept the Alfa on the road. The Maserati had lost ground.

134

At the bottom of the hill we came to more level ground. The bends were fast and sweeping. Here the faster car had the advantage. By the time we passed under the viaduct the Maserati had closed up to four hundred yards.

'Does this twit think he's going to follow us back to Rome?' Tro muttered, sparing a second glance in her mirror. 'I think it's time he had an accident.'

There was a right-angle bend ahead. At the apex on the outside a track led across fields to farm buildings. Tro took the corner far too fast. On the exit the back of the car spun through an extra hundred and eighty degrees. She controlled the spin perfectly, letting the rear end come to rest a yard from the ditch. She had kept the engine running. She selected first gear and accelerated round the corner and back up the road we had just come down. The manoeuvre had taken three seconds.

The Maserati's flat nose was now three hundred yards away. He had been chasing a car and now suddenly he found one coming towards him. Tro was holding the crown of the road. She changed up, kept increasing speed. The cars were now rushing towards each other at a meeting speed of one hundred and twenty miles an hour. It was like one of those games of Russian Roulette that Californian kids play on their long, straight highways to see who will chicken out first.

I wanted to look at Tro's face but my eyes were fixed in terror at the squat car bearing down on us. Its sloping front tapered to a blade-like edge. As the crash seemed imminent I waited for a swift death. But I did not close my eyes.

At the last instant the Maserati driver's nerve gave way. I never knew whether Tro's reactions would have been fast enough if he had not wrenched his wheel and careered off the road. He shot past our front wing, careering through a hedge and into a field.

Tro lost speed, did another handbrake turn. We drove back past the gap the Maserati had torn in the hedge. Through it I could see the car a hundred yards inside the field. It had ploughed a deep furrow but was still on all four wheels.

'That type is always chicken.' Tro's voice was scornful. 'I

doubt if he even realised we were the same car.' She looked round at me, laughing with pleasure. 'I think I shook him, don't you?'

'You bloody fool!' I burst out. 'You could have buggered up the whole job. Why the hell do you have to prove yourself the whole time?'

'Hey!' she protested.

'We were trying to make ourselves *in*conspicuous. Now everyone in Capretto will be talking about this.'

She took the right-angle bend more soberly this time. Black marks on the road surface showed where she had spun the car.

'He was following us. I got rid of him, didn't I?'

'No Italian can resist a dice with a pretty girl in a fast car. You stupid bitch.'

'Sod you!' said Tro.

'Stop the car, I'm driving from now on.'

'You bloody aren't.' She rammed the gear lever viciously into third.

I leaned forward and took the ignition key out.

'You bastard.'

Tro slipped into neutral. The car coasted to a halt.

I got out. We were on a deserted stretch of road with grassy banks on either side. Across a narrow strip of field the river fed from the hills behind was hastening towards the plain. I walked round to the passenger's side and yanked the door open. I was really angry.

'Out,' I said.

'Get stuffed.'

I leaned across and undid the seat belt. Then I dragged her by main force out of the car. She came with remarkably little resistance, but the moment she had her feet on the ground she aimed a vicious jab at my groin. I was ready for it. I blocked the blow and grabbed her wrist, forcing her up onto her toes. Her eyes sparked fire at me from six inches away. Her free hand jabbed at my face like a striking snake. Again I blocked her. She brought a knee up and I arched my waist backwards to save my genitals. That gave her a chance to break my hold.

She was a really dirty fighter, always going for the soft

targets. It took all my strength to get both her wrists behind her back and in the grip of one hand.

She glared at me, panting, her body squirmed against me. He open mouth was just below mine.

Suddenly the fight was over. She relaxed, pressed softly against me.

'Let go of my hands,' she whispered.

Still suspicious, I released her. But the tempo had changed. Changed completely. She put both her hands behind my head and pulled it down till our mouths met. My hands went round her body, one under the swell of her behind.

My head spun with the dizziness of the kiss. Our joined mouths were a sealed chamber where our tongues continued the duel that our bodies had abandoned. After a minute she tore her lips free. We were both breathing fast. The sense of urgency was mounting.

'It's going to be good,' she said. 'But not now, Patrick. And not here.'

EIGHT

Back in Rome at eleven o'clock we abandoned the hire car in the Corso and walked the rest of the way to Palazzo Mellini. We found a celebration in process.

Clement and Johnnie had gone to Pescara to follow up a strong lead that had been passed on by Peter, the undercover man at the British Embassy. They had indeed found a terrorist hide-out, but these were non-political gangsters operating purely for gain. They had liberated a child hostage.

'A *child* hostage?'

'Yes. A girl of twelve.' Johnnie's face darkened. 'God, the state she was in. Tied hands and feet to a bed with a gag in her mouth for two months. The only time they let her loose was to rape her. People who do that to a kid don't deserve to live.'

'Well, they didn't, did they?' Clement said quietly.

'You mean, you killed them?' It was Tro who asked the unnecessary question.

'If we hadn't they'd have killed the girl,' Johnnie told her. 'Jesus, if you'd seen her! We dropped her off at the local nunnery.'

Those terrorists never had much chance. Clement and Johnnie had gone out like a couple of mastiffs intent on a kill. They had needed to do something to counter-balance the shooting of Franco.

The story of the mysterious double assassination in the Foro Romano was in all the evening papers. The macabre discovery that a male corpse lay under the nun's habit had fired the imagination of the editors. He had been identified as a suspected member of the Red Brigades. The identity of the second victim was not yet known.

I asked Richie if he had told Franco's wife yet.

'No, old Pat. I can't do anything about that without

compromising the job. I'm not looking forward to it. She's a sweet person.'

He shook his head. Then, with one of those sudden changes of mood that were typical of him, he quizzed Tro and me. The old grin was on his face.

'Well, how did the honeymoon couple get on? You can drop the act now, you know.'

Maybe Richie had only one eye but it did not miss much. Since the tussle by the roadside Tro and I had been treating each other with studied casualness. All the same there was a subtle change in her. She was somehow less brittle, more lissome.

I filled Richie in on our visit to Capretto and what we had found there. I did not mention the dice with the Maserati.

'The only problem is, how did they get in there?' I finished. 'It's inaccessible to vehicles.'

'Could have used a chopper,' Clement said, from his usual place in the doorway. 'They didn't want to attract attention they'd auto-rotate down.'

I explained for Tro's benefit. 'You can land a helicopter without the engines by letting the blades act like a parachute. Like those seeds you see spinning to earth in autumn. Takes a skilled pilot to do it.'

'There was no sign of any helicopter,' she objected.

'Could have been hidden,' Clement observed. 'You said there were several other buildings.'

There had been some strange characters nosing around the Palazzo that day. Richie was insisting more than ever that we should never move outside the Palazzo alone. The rooms at the Albergo Luna had been given up. We would all stay in Franco's flat with a permanent watch in the courtyard below. Palazzo Mellini was becoming more and more like a fortress in the centre of Rome. The patient Stan had been saddled all day with the job of standing guard, using the wine store as a kind of sentry-box.

'Problem is,' Richie said, 'if vehicles can't get into that hide-out, how do we get there? You can't arrive surreptitiously by helicopter, always supposing we could get

139

hold of one.'

'There's a town called Sasso on the northern side of the range behind Pian di Capretto. We did a detour round there after we'd — ah — made our exit from Capretto.'

I took care not to look at Tro. She got up and went into the kitchen.

'It's a long way round, but when you reach it you're only about five miles from Capretto. The road ends at Sasso and there's not even a track over the mountains. But I think it might be possible to get over with a car, especially as we have four-wheel drive. After all, Hannibal got his elephants over the Alps.'

I spread the 1:50,000 map of the area out on the table. The hachuring indicated that the terrain was fearsome, but I showed him a possible route I had worked out. It passed between the peaks of Monte Calvo and Monte Vergine. We were poring over it when Tro came back with cups of coffee and slices of Motta cake.

'You haven't said anything about Lady S,' she reminded Richie.

'We haven't wanted to use the 'phone too much. I telephoned the Hotel Churchill from the Albergo at about six. She wasn't there and the Embassy didn't know where she'd gone. They were getting a bit worried about her.'

Tro banged the tray down with a crash. 'For Christ's sake! Why didn't you tell me this before? Anything may have — '

'You think the sun rises and sets out of Lady S's ass.' Richie retorted. 'Dammit, I had Clem and Johnnie coming back with the blood of three terrorists on their hands and expecting the police to turn up at any moment about Franco. Lady S came out here on her own initiative. She can't expect us to nanny her.'

'I'm going to ring the hotel, okay?' Tro said defiantly. 'Just to see if she's all right. I mean, she's been alone all day.'

Richie and I remained silent while she went to telephone. I could feel him studying me cannily. We heard Tro speak a few staccato sentences in Italian. Then she crashed the receiver down.

140

'I could only get the reception desk.' She hurried past us towards the door of the flat. 'They say she came in about an hour ago but there's no reply from her room. I'm going round there.'

'Hold it!' Richie jumped to his feet to intercept her. 'Nobody goes out of the Palazzo alone. That's the rule.'

'Then Patrick can come with me, okay?'

Life was going on as normal at the Hotel Churchill. Guests returning from theatres and restaurants were collecting their keys from the porters' desk. A party of late arrivals were checking in at the reception desk. Their luggage, decked with airline dockets, was piled in the foyer behind them. A vociferous party was just coming out of the cocktail bar, young people in amorous mood warming up for a night on the town — or on each other.

These symptoms of normality only increased Tro's impatience. She had to throw a big show of temperament to stir the staff into action. Luckily one of the receptionists remembered her from her prevous visit. At last we were taken up to Lady Stewart's suite by a bell-boy with a pass key.

The suite was empty. After two nights of calls the flow of information had petered out. The telephonist and the detective had returned to normal duties. But the tape-recording system was still in place.

I searched for clues as to where Lady Stewart might have gone. Her bedroom was untidy, the wardrobe doors gaping and drawers left open. There were other signs that she had left in a hurry. But not long ago. The loo had been used recently.

I went back to the sitting-room. Tro was sitting at the tape-recorder.

'There's a conversation on the tape. I'm just winding it back.'

It took her a couple of minutes to locate the beginning of the last conversation, preceded by the usual ringing tone. I was standing behind her as the recorded conversation crackled out of the speaker.

'Milady Stewart?'

'Yes. Who is that speaking?'

'A friend. You would like to see your husband again?'

The voice was male and sounded fairly old. He spoke in slow, careful English.

'Yes,' Lady Stewart replied. 'Who are you? Where are you speaking from?'

'I know where he is. I can take you there.' The caller continued his message, ignoring her question. He had prepared his little speeches and was not geared to dealing with unscripted queries. 'You have money?'

'I have twenty million. That is all I have been able to collect.'

'Twenty million lire?' The anonymous caller sounded surprised, perhaps that so little was available for a ransom.

'Yes.'

There was a pause.

'Come with the money to the column in Piazza Colonna at midnight exactly. Come alone. On foot. Tell no one. If you speak to anyone you will never see your husband again. You understand?'

'Yes. How will I know you?'

'You will not. But I will know you.'

There was a click, followed by Lady Stewart's voice calling: 'Wait! Hello! . . . Hello! . . .' Then the receiver went down, ending the recording.

'God!' I gasped. 'She didn't fall for that old trick! What time is it?'

'Seven minutes to midnight.'

'Come on!'

We rushed out of the flat and along the corridor. The lifts were patiently tagging up and down the six-storey building, their bells resounding in the shaft with maddening complacency. We ran to the stairs and careered down them two or three at a time. In the foyer we pushed through the groups that were standing chatting idly. The revolving doors clattered hysterically as we rammed violently through them.

I had left the Saab by the kerb outside. A *vigile* was contemplating it gloomily. He was already reaching for the leather-bound wallet of forms to book us.

'*Momento!*' he shouted, as we opened the doors and flung ourselves in.

'English,' Tro shouted at him. '*Non capito.*'

I was behind the wheel, firing up the engine. I built up some boost before letting the clutch in. I squirted the car out into the traffic moving fast down Via XX Settembre.

'Whoever they are they're amateurs,' I said, moving into the centre of the road and building up speed. The turbo charger came in with its discreet whine. I switched the hazard warning lights on. 'Professionals would never choose a pick-up point like that.'

If Rome has a centre it is Piazza Colonna. The Column itself stands in the centre of a square enclosed on three sides by colonnaded buildings.

Holding second gear for higher revs and maximum boost I hurled the Saab to the right through the Piazza Quirinale and dived towards a small street running westward. I must have violated some sacred precinct. Behind me a challenge rang out, followed by a shot. But by then I was long gone.

'Time?'

'Just on midnight.'

I thrust up past the Trevi fountain, using my sense of direction to work down towards the Via del Corso. Once I found myself going the wrong way up a Senso Unico street. Outraged motorists hooted and flashed their lights at me. I blazed back at them. The car lurched as the right-hand wheels mounted the pavement. Pedestrians leaped for cover in doorways as we passed.

By good luck we burst into Via del Corso bang opposite Piazza della Colonna. I barged out into the traffic, forcing other vehicles to stop and give me passage. Italians don't like that sort of thing but fortunately they have good brakes.

'God! God!' Tro was mouthing, as cars screeched to a halt a few feet from our flanks.

The ancient column rose yellowy-grey in the centre of the piazza ahead of us. I drove straight for it, knocking over a barrier that had been placed to exclude traffic from the area.

In a tight circle I drove the three hundred and sixty degrees round the column. There was nobody. The dashboard clock told me that it was two minutes after midnight.

I did a wider tour, Tro and I both searching the colonnades for any sign of an elderly lady with a heavy suitcase.

We were too late.

There was a little convoy on my tail, angry drivers who had been scared into fury by my street tactics. It would have been a mistake to try and argue with so many.

I drove out into the Via and used the hurtling acceleration of the Turbo to lose them.

'So much for the lady's extra-sensory perceptions,' Richie commented when I told him what had happened. 'She really walked into that one.'

'We don't know that yet,' Tro said angrily. 'Perhaps the person does know where the General is.'

Richie shook his head pityingly. 'It was some crook on the make. He's collected twenty million and now he'll demand as much again as a ransom. We'll pass this buck to Peter, and the Italian police can follow it up.'

Johnnie went down to the courtyard to relieve Stan and give him a well-earned respite. The ex-PATU man had a lot of experience of anti-terrorist patrols in rough country. His skills would be useful in the Hannibal-type operation we would be undertaking in the savage mountainous country north of Florence. As he had missed my report Richie and I went over the ground again for his benefit, with the 1:50,000 *Istitutio Geografico Militare* map spread out before us.

'Why take cars at all?' Stan said. 'You're much better on foot in this sort of country.'

'We're going to want the surveillance equipment as well as our weapons. That stuff weighs a hell of a lot. Besides, though we can't approach up the road from Capretto we hope to get out that way.'

In order to enable us to move away without delay as soon as a positive message came through, the gear was transferred from the wine store to the cars. While everybody else went back to the flat to fit in some sleep, Johnnie was left to stand watch in the courtyard. I would relieve him in an hour and a half at 2.30.

The five of us tossed an English coin to decide who would have the only two beds in Franco's flat. Richie and Stan won. Clement, Tro and I made ourselves as comfortable as we could in the sitting-room. I set the alarm on my wrist-watch to wake me at 2.25.

It was an optimistic gesture. I found myself quite unable to sleep, a most unusual circumstance for me. Through the closed door of the bedroom I could hear Stan snoring rhythmically. It would take more than that to disturb Richie. Clement was stretched full length on the carpet with a cushion under the back of his neck. He had the capacity to go out like a light the moment he closed his eyes. Tro was curled up on the sofa with one hand tucked between her thighs. I could not see her face, so there was no way of telling whether she was asleep or awake.

I was in the two chairs that Richie had occupied the night before.

The area round the Palazzo was quiet compared with the rest of Rome. I could hear the distant murmur of traffic in the main streets. In the nearby alleys individual sounds punctuated the stillness sharply and in a way were more disturbing than continuous noise. I could hear a man coughing drily in a nearby house. A woman's laughter bubbled up and was hushed. The silence was briefly raped by a motor scooter racing past. Cats squabbled viciously round the dustbins and somewhere in the distance a burglar alarm was ringing unheeded. From one of the other flats in the palazzo came the thud-thud of rock music played on a hi-fi rig with a very strong bass loudspeaker.

Half asleep, my brain rummaged among the crowded memories of the four days that had passed since that first night message from Richie. When you're dozing your mind lurches illogically from one picture to another. I saw myself standing again in front of the gravestone in the cemetery at Cassino. My imagination conjured up the skeleton of General

Stewart's younger brother. I wondered whether he had yet crumbled into dust.

The picture of Lady Stewart materialised before my closed eyes, tied like the girl of twelve in a filthy hovel with a gag stuffed in her mouth. Goodbye to that dignity and charm.

And the General, now one hundred hours into his captivity. Had he talked yet? Were the secrets of the British Independent Satellite-based Attack System already on their way to the Intelligence experts of the Russian High Command?

Mixed in with it all, like the refrain at the end of a hymn with too many verses, was the elusive and ever-changing image of Tro. I lived again that wild moment when our mouths collided and our bodies screamed silently to each other.

These conscious thoughts gradually melted into the stuff of dreams. I saw myself with Tro. We were naked, our bodies wrapped together being carried along by a sparkling warm stream. There was no gravity except the force pulling our two bodies together. We tumbled weightless in water that bubbled like champagne . . .

The bleep on my wrist-watch woke me in the nick of time.

Enough light from a street lamp came through a chink in the shutters for me to find my shoes and anorak. Clement and Tro did not waken as I put them on. I took my Browning from under the cushion which had served as a pillow.

I let myself out of the flat and went down the stone stairs. A chink of light showed under the door of Flat 3, the one beneath Franco's. It had been empty since our arrival. The occupants must have come back from the country that day.

The only illumination in the courtyard came from the dim bulbs on the stairways leading to the flats and the beam of a street lamp slanting through the entrance archway. The parked cars were black humps. The branches and leaves of the jasmine made dark patterns against a blue-black sky. The squirting jet spattered feebly on the water of the fountain.

There was no light on in the store. Johnnie would not want to place himself at the disadvantage of having a light behind him. I could imagine him sitting or standing just inside the doorway with his gun within reach.

I called his name quietly as I walked across the cobbles. I did not want him to mistake me for an intruder. There was no answer. I called softly again as I came nearer.

'Johnnie?'

The door of the wine depot was closed. I opened it. Darkness inside. I switched the light on and searched behind the piles of cartons, not really expecting to find that Johnnie had fallen asleep while on watch.

Perhaps he was doing a sentry's beat, patrolling the perimeter. I went to the archway and stared out. The street running down to the Corso was deserted except for one figure hurrying along close by the walls of the houses. He stopped and turned to stare back. I took him for one of the *teppisti* who roam the streets in search of suitable victims for mugging.

Back inside the courtyard I made a tour of the square enclosure, checking inside the three doorways that led to flats or maisonettes. I had almost got back to our two cars parked ready outside the store when my foot slipped on a viscous substance on the cobbles. I switched on my torch to examine it. There was a dark pool and a trail leading towards the jasmine beside the fountain. Something had been dragged across the ground.

I stooped and took a sample on my finger tip. I put it to my nose. Blood.

I followed the wet trail towards the jasmine. Other plants had taken root round its trunk forming a patch of untidy, tangled undergrowth. This vegetation had been flattened when a heavy body had been dragged in there.

Feet first. The head was the first thing I saw. He had been killed by one of his own favourite methods, the garrot. His eyes, still wide open, had almost popped out of their sockets. A blue tongue poked obscenely from the gaping mouth. I switched the torch off quickly. I had seen enough of that terrible caricature of a human countenance.

I squatted there in the dark, adjusting to the shock and the nausea. It took me a minute or so. I was just straightening up

147

when I heard the slither of a footstep. It came from the doorway to the stairs leading to Franco's flat. I caught a quick glimpse of a form outlined against the light inside. Then it blended with the darkness.

Moving fast I was just in time to intercept him as he reached the archway. When I flashed the torch on him he stopped, terrified. He was a young man of about twenty, wearing a Levi jacket and trousers. The handles of a pair of pliers protruded from one of the jacket pockets. His face was pitted with acne scars.

'Who are you?' I asked him in Italian.

'I — ah. I'm the boy friend of the girl in Flat Three.'

'You mean Maria?'

'That's right.'

'Her name's not Maria. It's Anna.'

The bluff worked. I expected him to contradict me and brazen it out. He did not try to keep up the pretence. He made a sudden dash for the archway. I kicked at his ankle. His foot caught the back of his calf and he went down with a crash. I was right behind him. While his limbs were still loose from the fall I grabbed his left arm and put a wrist lock on him.

He squealed with pain. I brought him to his feet. His left elbow was against my chest, the wrist doubled over beneath my hand. Pressure brought excruciating agony. He was dancing on tiptoe, gasping and pleading with me to let him go. Perhaps I was a little impervious to his suffering. The picture of Johnnie's face was still stark before my eyes.

'You're coming back upstairs with me,' I told him. 'And stop yelling or I'll break your wrist.'

Despite the pain he was reluctant to come. There was some very urgent reason impelling him to get away from the place. I thought it was the knowledge that a dead body lay under the jasmine. As I dragged him to the stairway to Flats 3 and 4 he was still begging me to let him go. Twice on the stairs he risked a broken wrist in an attempt to wriggle away from me.

I had closed the flat door coming out. Johnnie had a key to let himself in but it was still in his pocket. I hammered on the door.

Clement came to open it. His protest died when he saw my captive.

'What have we here?'

'I'm not sure, but I think he may have killed Johnnie.'

'*What*?'

'Johnnie's dead. He's been garrotted. He's down there under the tree by the fountain.'

Clement pushed past me, went racing down the stairs. I dragged my captive into the flat, kicked the door shut with my foot.

Tro was struggling into wakefulness as I brought him into the sitting-room. Richie and Stan had heard the commotion. They came bursting out of the bedroom, Richie with his flies undone and a grisly hollow where his glass eye should have been.

In a few quick sentences I told them what had happened. Richie made to go after Clement but I stopped him.

'There's something odd about this chap. He's absolutely gibbering with terror and for some reason he has a hysterical compulsion to get away from here. I think we ought to get him talking — and pretty quick too.'

'No problem,' Stan said, giving the youth a quick, assessing inspection. 'Put him on that chair and tie his hands behind it.'

The youth was blubbering as I set him on the chair. I fed his arms to Richie who tied his crossed wrists with a length of nylon cord. He passed the free ends under the seat of the chair and knotted them over our prisoner's thighs.

Stan took the pliers from his pocket and examined them. They were the kind electricians use for minor repairs.

'These will do fine. You ask the questions and I'll do the persuading.'

He pulled the Levi jacket open. The Beretta automatic was tucked into his waistbelt. He had been too panic-stricken to use it. Stan removed it and handed it to me with a wry grin. He ripped the man's shirt apart. The buttons flew off and skeetered across the boards. Stan applied the pliers to one of the bared nipples.

I said, reverting to Italian: 'Who killed my friend down in

149

the courtyard? Was it you?'

'No. No. It was Antonio.'

'Where is he now?'

'He's gone. I was left to — I'm telling you the truth, let me go, let me go — '

'What were you doing in the flat down below? It's been empty for the last four days.'

'I know, I know! Holy Mary, Mother of God! Let me go! I beg you!'

'How many of you are there? Why did you come here?'

'What's the time? What's the time?'

'Don't worry about the time. What were you after, you and Antonio?'

He was fighting the cord in panic, hardly heeding Stan's poised pliers.

'The time, what is it?'

'Why are you so concerned about the time?'

'There's a bomb in the flat below!'

'*God*!' Richie exploded. 'When is it timed to go off?'

The Italian had not understood. I repeated the question.

'A quarter to three. Please, let me go now. I've told you the truth.'

All four of us whipped our wrists up to look at our watches.

'Four minutes,' Richie said. 'Ask him how much explosive.'

I fired the question at the bound man.

'Fifteen pounds of plastic.'

'Christ! That's enough to blow the whole Palazzo sky high! Come on, we've got to get out of here.'

Stan made no move. 'We can't just leave all the people in these flats. There are kids too.' He jerked his head at the feverishly struggling Italian. 'You lot get the hell out. I'll take chummy down to the flat below and we'll defuse it.'

'Look at the state he's in,' Richie said. ''Sides, you haven't got time.'

Stan moved towards the Italian. 'He may be bluffing. It's worth a try.'

'Stan!' Richie shouted peremptorily. 'I can't spare you. *The*

150

job comes first. Now, you look after Tro. Get her down to the cars and warn Clem.'

For an instant it seemed that Stan might refuse. Then he looked at Tro. She was standing as if paralysed. He grabbed her by the arm and headed for the front door.

Richie had dived back into the bedroom. I was about to follow Stan and Tro when I remembered the car keys. I'd put them down somewhere in the hall. I was looking for them when Richie came storming past me. He had the case with his glass eye in one hand and the suitcase with the billion lire in the other.

'Come on, Patrick! What the hell are you waiting for?'

'The car keys. Ah. Here they are.'

The keys of the Audi as well as the Saab's were lying under the 1:50,000 map of the Capretto area. I scooped up keys and map.

Behind us in the sitting-room the young terrorist was howling. *'Mamma mia* — you're not going to leave me. For the love of God — '

'You shouldn't plant bombs,' Richie flung back at him.

We raced down the stairs. There was no time to warn the occupants of the other flats. At the tops of our voices we yelled: *'Bomba! Bomba! Tutti fuori!'*

In the courtyard Clement, warned by Stan, was coming out of the store. The light in there was on, throwing the two cars parked outside into relief. Clement had carried Johnnie's body in and laid it down among the wine cases.

Tro stared at me, her face chalky in the gloom.

'The car keys! I forgot them!'

'Catch.' I tossed her the keys of the Audi. They glinted in the light from the store as they curved through the air. She caught them with both hands like a slip fielder.

The luminous dial of my watch showed me that it was 2.43 by Italian radio time. If the terrorists' timing was accurate we had two minutes to go. Lights were going on in the windows overlooking the courtyard. Through some of them heads were being poked out.

'What's happening? What's happening?'

'Get back from the windows,' I yelled. 'There's a bomb. Lie on the floor under the windows.'

There was nothing more we could do for them. From the stairway behind us came an awful clattering noise. The terrorist, still tied to his chair, was trying to get down the stairs. I heard him lose balance and crash down, screaming.

I was already at the door of the Saab. Stan, Clement and Tro had piled into the Audi. I slid in and leaned across to unfasten the lock on Richie's side. He came in beside me, hauling the suitcase after him. There was just space for him to balance it on his knee as he slammed the door.

I pushed the ignition key into the socket between the two front seats and turned it. The engine fired at once, running on the automatic choke. As I came out of reverse and selected first gear the Audi shot across the front of my bows. Tro was holding a four-wheel power slide as she catapulted the Quattro through the archway.

I let in my clutch and followed her, the front wheels slipping on the cobbles as they fought for grip. The rear end clouted the side of the archway as we rocked through it. At the bottom of the ramp leading down from the Palazzo the front suspension bottomed. I aimed for the nearest available street opening and bombed into it. The Audi was a hundred yards ahead.

Beside me, Richie was taking his glass eye from its case and fitting it into place.

Then the night sky was lit by an orange flash from behind us. The earth pulsed with a tremor that could be felt through the suspension of the car. An instant later came the concussion of a gigantic explosion.

NINE

The sun rising from behind the dark green of the Chianti hills
caught us on the old road from Siena to Florence. We were
headed for Capretto. There was really nowhere else for us to
go.

Beside me Richie leaned forward and picked up the mike of
the CB radio.

'You on channel, ex-colonial?'

'Yeah, go ahead, goodbuddie,' Stan answered from the
Audi.

'Tell me something, did you or Sharpshooter put the
Cortex on board?'

'The Cortex? Tubby was going to do that.'

'Well, I hope he did. Listen, we'll stop in Florence for
breakfast and a ten one hundred.'

'Roger D.'

The CB radios had fully justified themselves. After baling
out of the Palazzo in such haste the first priority had been to
put distance between ourselves and the explosion. Richie had
been able to talk to Tro, directing her towards the banks of the
Tiber and out of Rome onto the Viterbo road. He'd decided to
avoid the autostrada and follow what had been the old route of
the Mille Miglia. The police were bound to set up road blocks
after such a massive terrorist outrage. The autostrada was too
obvious an escape route. And there's no way you can
circumvent a road block on the autostrada.

Viterbo is fifty miles from Rome. On almost empty roads
we'd reached it in half an hour, rivalling the speeds of
competitors in Italy's defunct road race. We'd passed Siena as
the dawn light etched the towers round Piazza del Campo
against the sky. No road blocks. The chances were that they
were being put up behind us.

We had no problem parking in Florence. It was still early.

Even the attendants of the *parcheggios* were not yet on duty. There was a café open on the Lungarno, just over the Ponte San Niccolo.

It was a silent and thoughtful group of four men and a woman who sat round a plastic-topped table eating over-boiled eggs and drinking relays of cups of capuccino. The other customers were working people stopping on their way in to Florence.

With one cup of coffee inside him Richie went to telephone Peter. I don't think any of us said a single word while we waited for him to come back. The impact of Johnnie's death and our narrow escape from fragmentation precluded small talk.

'Rome is in a state of panic,' Richie said when he rejoined us. 'That explosion was heard all over the city. People think it heralds the attack the Red Brigades have been threatening on the centres of government. Peter was sure we'd gone sky-high with Palazzo Mellini.'

'Were there — were many people killed?'

'Nobody knows how many yet, Tro. They're still searching the wreckage.'

'Those kids!'

'Yes. I know.' Something other than the slaughter of innocent victims was on Richie's mind. 'Peter told me we were to pack it in. Apparently Charles is getting cold feet.'

I was watching Tro's face. She was white and strained but I was sure the expression I surprised was one of disappointment.

Clement chewed hard and swallowed his bread. 'What did you answer?'

'I said I'd think about it.'

Stan said: 'Now that we've found the hide-out for them would it not be better to let the Italians tackle it? They are better equipped to deal with a situation like that than we are.'

'No way,' Richie snapped angrily. It was the second time Stan had suggested handing the operation over. 'This is our operation. I'm not going to let anyone else take if from me now.'

'Fair enough,' Stan began. 'I just thought — '

Richie put a hand up to stop him. It was seven-thirty and the news bulletin was coming through on the café's radio.

The explosion in Rome was the principal item, as it had been since the first news-flash at 3 am. One whole side of Palazzo Mellini had been reduced to rubble and much of the rest had been consumed in the ensuing conflagration. The rescue work was still proceeding. Seven bodies had already been recovered. Mystery surrounded the motive for the outrage. It was now being suggested that this was part of a vendetta between rival terrorist groups of the extreme right and the extreme left.

Even the East-West crisis had been relegated to second place but the symptoms were ominous. A United States satellite in geostationary orbit 22,000 miles above the equator had been destroyed. The American National Intelligence Agency believed that its destruction had been caused by a laser beam from a manned Soviet space craft.

Colonna Nuova had issued a fresh communiqué. It had irrefutable proof that *Colonna Nuova* suspects arrested by the police had been tortured during interrogation. Unless their demands for the release of all CL detainees were met within twenty-four hours the *Generalissimo* would be executed by order of a People's Court.

'They must be getting desperate,' Stan commented, as the radio was turned down. 'When they start setting deadlines you know they've lost confidence.'

Clement looked at him thoughtfully. He took a toothpick from the holder in the middle of the table and began to dislodge the bits of crust that had stuck in his gums. I could not read his expression. I had long ago given up trying to guess what went on in Clement's mind.

We had to kill time till the shops opened. Tro and I went to a supermarket to buy provisions for a couple of days in the mountains. Richie took Stan with him up to the area of expensive shops between the Piazza Signoria and the Duomo. Clement was left to watch the cases.

We were all three waiting at the car park when Richie and

155

Stan returned. They were festooned with cine cameras and photographic equipment.

On the way out of Florence we stopped at a tyre specialist's to have narrow-section cross-country Pirelli tyres fitted to both cars.

The sun was high when we crossed the Futa Pass and took the turning that led to Sasso. As the road climbed towards the town at the head of the valley Richie was staring at the mountains rising steeply behind it.

'You didn't tell me we had to drive up a bloody precipice.'

We made no attempt to cut a low profile in Sasso. The cars were parked outside the café in the main square, the cine equipment plainly visible on the back seats. We all went inside for a beer. Chatting to the bar-tender and any interested locals we let it be known that we were a television crew filming some shots of cars negotiating difficult terrain. A little crowd collected to watch us drive away. There was no shortage of advice on how to get up into the hills.

Tro in the Audi led. I followed at the wheel of the Saab. We had ten hours of daylight left. The saddle between the peaks of Monte Calvo and Monte Vergine was three thousand feet above us.

The first part of the climb was fairly simple. There were still working farms above the town. The tracks leading to them were in good condition. Beyond that was a belt which had once been farmed but had been abandoned after the great migration from the country to the cities. Here the tracks had fallen into disrepair. The going was rough but no worse than you'd expect on a rally. Soon after the last of the derelict farm buildings the ground dipped beyond a false crest. Through the dip ahead a busy stream flowed fast over a stony bed.

I took my shoes, socks and trousers off and waded into the ice-cold water. It was deeper than it looked. Rummaging among the spares in the boot of the Saab I found enough flexible tubing to jury-rig extensions that raised the exhaust emission point to the level of the boot lid. On the engine it was simple to pull the warm-air intake pipe off and stick it just under the bonnet.

Once through the pine forest above the stream the mountains became bare. The gradient varied from 1 in 1 to 1 in 3. We climbed five hundred feet by zig-zagging to and fro across the face of the mountain. With four-wheel drive and the differentials locked, Tro in the Audi had no problems. Given a run she could scramble up short slopes that looked almost vertical. Richie, Clement and Stan put their shoulders behind the Saab to help it up the steeper parts. The sun was warm now and they were soon sweating profusely.

We paused on a level shelf. Capretto was already more than a thousand feet below. Paradoxically the two peaks flanking the saddle we hoped to cross looked even higher from here. Richie had re-christened them Bare Arse and Black Tittie. The cleft betwen them had been dubbed Hooker's Crotch.

Thunder heads were building up over the Appenines to eastward. This brilliant sunshine was not going to last long.

Richie craned his neck to squint at the rock face ahead. Now that we were close underneath it this next section looked even more forbidding than from the valley. It towered above us, a grey wall of bare rock far steeper than the roof of a house. The average slope must have been sixty five degrees, more like the angle of a window-cleaner's ladder. The jagged summit outlined against the sky was four hundred feet overhead.

Even to reach the base of it was going to be a problem. After the narrow shelf on which we had stopped the slope became appreciably steeper. The Audi climbed it, bucking like a bronco, stones and earth flying back from all four wheels. The Saab's front driving wheels could not find enough purchase to grip, even with the cross-country Pirelli tyres. I had to turn her round and use reverse. With my ground crew pushing the bonnet we made it by fits and starts. It was largely thanks to Stan's colossal physical strength. He had been a front-row Rugby forward in Rhodesia.

By the time we came up level with Tro my three pushers were exhausted. Behind us sloping grey columns of rain were advancing up the valley. Capretto had already become invisible. A chill wind preceded the coming rainstorm.

157

Richie called a halt. We all crowded into the Saab to drink beer and eat some food. The rain struck us with the fury of a freak English storm, huge drops lashing the roof of the car. But unlike our home-grown storms it did not let up. The rain was still cascading down when we had finished eating.

It was two o'clock.

Clement stepped out, hunched under the rain. There was no view now. The peaks above us, even the saddle, were invisible. We only knew that we had to go on up.

'Never get cars up that.' Clement was staring gloomily at the rocky slope. 'We'll have to take the gear over on our backs.'

'We'll winch them up. It's going to take a bit of time, but —'

Among the equipment I had acquired from Bill Garland was a winch, used by mechanics to lift engines from cars. I hoped that the chain attached to it would take the weight of a car.

We decided to shift the Audi first. It was lighter and had four driving wheels to help. The heaviest items in the Saab, the weapons and metal spare parts, were loaded into the empty seats. The only human was Tro at the wheel.

We worked the Audi up the rock face in short stages. I would go ahead and fix the chain to an outcrop. Then I'd crank it up with Richie, Stan and Clement pushing the car from behind. The wheels bit at the surface, firing stones and fragments of rock back at the team of pushers. All the time the rain kept bucketing down. We were all soaked but working so hard that the moisture steamed off our bodies.

Then when the car was almost level with me we'd wedge the rear with rocks and I'd move the winch up to the next holding point. As we went higher the gradient increased to 70 degrees. At times the car seemed to be suspended in mid-air, supported only by the chain. If it snapped Stan, Clement and Richie would be crushed as it hurtled back down the slope.

It took three hours of hard labour to bully the Audi up those four hundred feet of rock — the engine racing and peaking as the wheels scrabbled for purchase or spun without adhesion, the men sweating, grunting and swearing, the storm lashing our bodies with slave-driving ferocity. We used our last ounce of strength to heave the car over the final crest. All four of us fell flat on our faces as the engine at last took up the strain. Ahead a more gentle slope led up towards Hooker's Crotch, still invisible above us.

All of us except Tro were exhausted. We stood with the rain stabbing icily at our bodies. There was nowhere to shelter on the mountain. Even the Audi was not available. It was crammed too full of gear. The car was an incongruous object standing on this inaccessible patch of ground. For sure, no wheeled vehicle had ever been up here before.

We rested for five minutes, panting and drinking rain.

'We learned a lot from that. I think we could get the Saab up too.'

Everyone except Richie looked at me with hatred.

'It's at least double the weight,' Stan pointed out. 'Will the chain stand it?'

'I guess the breaking strain is about ten tons. The Saab doesn't weigh as much as that and we'll put Tro in as driver again. She's the lightest of us.'

Three hours later the Saab stood beside the Audi at the top of the rock face. Completely bushed, we four men climbed into the empty seats and flaked out.

As we lay there the storm passed as suddenly as it had arrived. The sun came out, low now in the west. It was within an hour of its setting.

It was Tro's voice that stirred us.

'You'd better come and have a look at this.'

Richie and I struggled out of the front seats. Now that the storm had passed the surrounding landscape was etched clearly. Hooker's Crotch was only a hundred feet above us. Bare Arse and Black Tittie towered on either side. Sasso seemed to be almost vertically below. Its roofs still shone from the drenching rain.

Tro said: 'I've been up to the top.'

'What's it like on the other side?'

'That's why I said you'd better come and see.'

Richie gave her a sharp look. Her tone of voice was ominous.

The three of us trudged up to the top of the slope. Standing on the saddle we could see the rain columns drifting back down the valley on the other side. They had cleared Capretto already. As we watched, the viaduct over the autostrada materialised from the grey mist. Pian di Capretto was out of sight, shielded by a shoulder below Black Tittie. The road from Capretto could be seen snaking towards it, broken by the blurred patch of the avalanche.

It was what lay immediately in front of us that drew an oath from Richie.

Beyond Hooker's Crotch the valley plunged like the curving side of a tea-cup. It was lined with scree, a huge field of rock fragments ranging in size and shape from a football to a wine carton. Almost vertical at the top the gradient sloped out till it was no steeper than the staircase of a house.

Tro said: 'A stunt man drove a Renault 5 down from the top of Mont Blanc last year. There was a photo, you know, on the front page of *The Times*.'

'That was in snow,' I pointed out.

Tro pointed downwards. 'There's a sort of route that avoids the biggest rocks. If you could control the car sufficiently you might be able to avoid rolling.'

'Mm.'

'I mean "you" in a general sense. I'll go first with the Audi if you like.'

We brought the cars up to the saddle. Tro rummaged in the boot of the Saab for the two Griffin crash helmets Bill Garland had thrown in with the spares. She tossed one to me before putting her own on her head. I took it as an invitation to follow her if I could.

The others stood round making no comment as she strapped herself in very firmly with the rally-style shoulder harness fitted to the Audi. She hauled the strap up between her legs and snapped the three buckles into the quick-release catch on her stomach.

She started the engine up, checked that the forward and

central differentials were locked. Then she eased the Audi to the lip of the plunging chasm. I was reminded of a ski-jumper at the starting gate. Then the front of the Audi canted over the edge and the car began glissading down the precipitous slope. We could hear from the blip of the engine that she was keeping power on, rather as a yachtsman in a gale sets a storm sail to give himself steerage. The car went zig-zagging down the hill very fast, sliding and cavorting on the scree, often sideways. Somehow she was keeping it to the route she had chosen. It did not take long. She descended three hundred feet in about fifteen seconds. The run ended in a sideways slide on the grassy slope below the scree.

Tro opened the door and climbed out. She cupped her hands and shouted back.

'Piece of cake.'

The two sides of the chasm echoed her. 'Piece of cake. Piece of cake.'

I began to put on the crash helmet.

'We'll man-haul the surveillance gear,' Richie said hastily. 'It's a bit fragile for that sort of thing.'

'And take out the stun grenades,' Clement suggested. 'They explode on impact, remember.'

When he had unloaded what he wanted I climbed into the Saab. The safety belt was the touring pattern, much less effective than Tro's rally type. I fastened it and adjusted it carefully. At least there was no risk of collision with a vehicle coming the other way.

'When you get down, Pat,' Richie told me through the window, 'go on ahead and suss out the lie of the land. It's going to take us some time to bring all this gear down.'

As the bonnet went over the edge only the strap prevented me from falling onto the steering wheel. The car was almost vertical. The sensation as it plunged down was as thrilling as free-fall. I was already sliding sideways. Only by applying power could I maintain any sort of control, but that simply increased my rate of descent.

Only for the first part was I able to follow Tro's selected route, then the force of gravity took over. I lurched onto a scree of larger rocks. The whole side of the hill moved under me, the scree sliding. The bottom of the car thumped stones and the wheel jerked in my hands. Suddenly I was canted sideways. Through the window beside me I caught a quick flash of Tro standing by the Audi a long way below me. Then the car rolled and my small world went crazy. The seat belt held me but my helmet smashed against the metal door surrounds. In the boot the spare parts and weapons crashed against the lid and sides. I saw a cart-wheeling kaleidoscope of sky, hill and rocks. The din was deafening. The car went on rolling and rolling for what semed minutes on end.

At last, with a final thump it was still. It had come to rest lying on its side. I hung from the harness, head dangling. I could hear liquid trickling behind me. Petrol was escaping from the tank.

I was trying to extricate myself from the harness when the door over my head was opened, like a hatch. Mercifully it had not jammed. Tro's scared face peered in at me.

We tried to roll the Saab back onto all four wheels but our combined strength was not enough.

'You wait for the others, I'm going on ahead to see how far we are from the house.'

The sun had set and it was already gloomy down in this cleft in the mountains. Hooker's Crotch seemed a high precipice behind me. Black Tittie and Bare Arse struck high into the sky on either side. A grassy slope plunged steeply downwards. Five hundred feet lower the grass gave way to a forest of firs, the twin of the one on the other side. The semblance of a track followed the bottom of the valley beside a stream formed by the joining of a hundred rivulets. This had probably been sheep country once but with the flight from the hills it had been taken over by afforestation. These trees would not be mature for another ten years and then this old track would be up-graded to get the timber out.

Half way through the forest the sky lightened ahead of me. I came out into a flat open space which for some reason had not been planted. In the middle of it was an incongruous

162

concrete dome covered with moss. As I came round it I realised that it was an old German fort. It must have been built in 1944 by the Todt organisation as part of the Gothic Line. A square opening as big as a garage led through to the other side. Small ammunition chambers and stairways to the gun turrets opened off it.

Thirty-eight years ago those turrets had commanded a field of fire over the valley leading down to Capretto, but that view was now blocked by the forestry plantation.

I trotted on, but more cautiously. To judge by the contours of the hills above me I was coming near to Pian di Capretto. As the trees thinned ahead I slowed to a walk. Then, quite suddenly, I was at the edge of the shelf in the hills.

Ahead of me was a flat area of about three acres. At the far edge stood the chalet Tro and I had seen from Capretto, with its steeply pitched overhanging roof and its single chimney. There was just enough light for me to see that it was built of brick. The windows were all shuttered with thick planks. From here the door was not visible.

To my right were the old buildings of the mine. Their roofs had fallen in. Trees were growing out of them. Half a dozen black mouths gaped in the steep rock-face at the side of the flat area. Pairs of rusting rails led into the dark interiors.

Keeping under the trees I cautiously moved round till I could see the front of the chalet. The door was also shuttered from the outside. The battens had been nailed solidly into the wooden surround. The nails were new. As on all the windows a slit had been left between the middle battens. The purpose of those could be to provide peep-holes or, more probably, gun apertures. The chalet had been turned into a do-it-yourself fortress.

From here the approach road snaking up from the valley was visible. There were no marks of wheel tracks on it. No vehicle had come up here since the winter storms. The place was silent, deserted. Yet I still hesitated to venture out into the open.

Then an eerie thing happened.

From the chimney a thin, slightly quivering metal rod

emerged. It was pushed up till its tip was about ten feet above the chimney stack. I remembered Johnnie's comment when he was fitting CB radios to the cars that it was the aerial which counted.

It was not yet dark enough for me to risk approaching closer. Keeping under the trees I moved back till I was opposite a disused mine building about two hundred yards from the chalet. It obscured me from the chalet as I moved out across the open space.

This building was evidently a shed in which the vehicles used to transport the ore had been garaged. Its door showed signs of recent repair and was bolted. On the ground outside I noticed a pair of deep furrows. They led out to the middle of the flat area. There they ended, as mysteriously as the footsteps of a ghost in the snow.

I peered in through a window at the side. Ten feet from me I could just make out the gleaming fuselage of a helicopter. It was painted red and white. The single blade was folded back so that it was narrow enough to be pushed into quite a small shed. A set of snap-up dolly wheels had been fitted to the skids. By its shape and size I guessed it to be a Jet-Ranger.

I crouched there watching the chalet for five minutes, resisting the temptation to go closer. The aerial had been retracted. Around me the darkness closed in. Straining my ears I fancied I heard the sound of voices, low and monotonous. And once or twice a muffled shout.

Moved by a sudden sense of urgency I straightened up and headed back through the forest. It was so dark under the trees that I had to use the sound of the stream as a guide to direction.

As I approached the clearing I saw the dancing yellow flames of a fire ahead. The others had followed me down as far as the fort. They had rolled the Saab onto all four wheels but it was unsteerable so they had abandoned it. The Audi had been driven under the square archway. Stan had searched out easily combustible twigs and branches to get a fire going. Richie and Clement were trying to dry their soaked clothes. The gear and weapons had been unpacked and laid out along the wall. An inspection lamp powered from the car battery hung from a ring on the wall.

I told Richie what I'd seen. He questioned me closely on the construction of the house and the battens on the windows and door.

'We left the Cordex and detonators behind,' he told me. 'I guess Johnnie was going to put them in just before we left.'

'So we have no explosive?'

'No.'

'What about the stun grenades?'

Clement shook his head. 'They just make a bang. No real blast effect.'

'We'll shelve that problem for the moment,' Richie said. 'We have seven hours of darkness. It's just possible we could spring him before daylight. The first thing is to find out what's going on inside that house.'

'Mind if I go back and see if I can get the Saab going?'

'Why bother with the Saab? We don't need it any more. We carried all the gear down with us.'

'If you've no explosive we could use it as a battering ram. That car's strong enough to punch a hole through a brick wall.'

Richie looked at me thoughtfully.

'Right, you do that, old Pat.'

I watched them load themselves up with the surveillance equipment. Richie and Clement between them carried the bulky audio-visual monitor. Stan humped the external suction mikes and the extension amplifier. Tro took the thermal sensors and both pairs of image intensifying goggles. Each of them had a hand-gun but the other weapons and grenades were left in the fort.

It took me an hour and a half to put the Saab to rights. The front wishbone had been seriously distorted. On the soft uneven ground the standard type of jack was useless. Bill Garland's kit included one of the bag-type jacks inflated from the car's exhaust. It raised the front of the Saab sufficiently for me to crawl under and remove the wishbone. Half an hour's energetic work with a heavy hammer on a flat rock got it straightened out well enough for me to refit it. Conditions were not conducive to a precision job. I was lying in soggy grass with only the light of the inspection lamp to work by.

When I'd finished, the Saab was a serviceable though very battered object. I used sidelights to follow the Audi's wheel marks as far as the track, then on down to the old fort.

Richie had said he'd send Tro back to contact me but she had not returned. I put some more wood on the fire and it soon flared up, casting its yellow light on the walls of the square tunnel. I wondered whether the guns that had been positioned here had ever been fired in anger. Curious to find out how much of the installation had been left behind, I began an exploration of the stairways leading up from the central tunnel. At the bottom of each was a small chamber. In the second one my torch picked up a makeshift bed. There were empty food tins in one corner and some very basic cooking utensils. On the floor were half a dozen cigarette stubs, smoked down to the bitter end. I picked one up and smelled it. The tobacco was acrid but fresh.

Someone else was using the old fort as a base.

A minute later I found out the reason why. In a third chamber there were piles of fresh moss, moistened by a drip from the leaking ceiling. These were exotic mountain mosses, the kind that are prized by city flower shops. The moss-gatherer probably made regular trips up from Capretto to collect his mosses for despatch to Florence or Rome.

Out near the fire I heard a cough and the sound of a footstep. I extinguished the torch and went out to the doorway. A figure was standing between me and the fire. He turned and I realised it was Stan.

'We're not the only people using this fort,' I told him. 'Some moss-gatherer is using it as a store.'

'Richie wants you down there at once.' Stan was not interested in moss-gatherers. 'We're to bring the rest of the gear in the Saab and stop about a hundred yards from the clearing.'

'What's happening down there?'

'They've already located the General, thanks to the external

166

mikes. He's in a cellar at the back of the house. When I left
Clem was drilling a hole through the outside wall of the
living-room the terrorists are using — '

'How many of them are there?'

'As far as we can tell from the thermal sensors and the
voices there's three men and a woman. She's an English
speaker and doing most of the interrogation. From what we've
heard they're giving the General a bad time.'

We loaded the weapons and grenades that had been left
behind into the Saab. I started her off on the engine, then
switched it off and coasted down quietly till we were just short
of the flat shelf of Pian di Capretto.

Richie and Stan were in one of the disused mine buildings.
The leads from the external microphones came through the
window to an amplifier fitted with head-phones. Tro was
listening intently to the sounds coming through on the head-
set. Another lead was connected to the small TV screen of the
audio-visual monitor. It was still dead.

'We've worked out what's going on inside the house,'
Richie told me in a whisper. 'There are two bedrooms on the
far side. On this side is the living-room. Between them is an
entrance hall with a bathroom opening off the far end of it.
There's a kitchen and store at the back, connecting with the
living-room. Below the store is a cellar. We think there's a
doorway and a flight of steps going down. That's where
they've got the General.'

'In the cellar?'

'Yes. The terrorists spend most of their time in the living-
room. None of them are sleeping, not tonight anyway.
They're not using the bedrooms. They seem to be on a count-
down. Tro has the impression that they're under orders from
outside to kill the General when the deadline expires and
they're not happy about it. They're getting desperate,
stepping up their interrogation. We have a mike clamped to
the wall low down as near as we can to the cellar. That's what
Tro's listening to. Clem is boring a hole with a hand-drill
through to that living-room . . .'

Tro took her head-set off and handed it to me.

'Listen to that.'

'What's happening?'

'If you listen carefully you'll hear a woman's voice. She's down with the General, interrogating him.'

I put the head-set on. The noises were very confused, like a radio with a lot of interference. There were men's voices talking near at hand. But in the gaps I could hear the voice of the woman and then the babbling replies, like a child speaking with an adult's voice. Straining my ears I tried to make some sense of it. Only odd phrases from the woman were audible. 'Phase of the battle . . . tactical nuclear weapons . . . satellite-based laser . . . nuclear release procedure.'

It was evidently an interrogation of a highly military and technical nature being carried out by an expert, or someone briefed by an expert. The replies were more confused. I hardly believed my ears when I heard the man's voice say, with sudden clarity:

'Who is the happy warrior, who is he? That every man in arms should WISH TO BE . . .' The last words were uttered in a shout of desperation or pain. 'It is the generous spirit, who, when brought among the tasks of real life . . .'

'Are they initials?' the woman broke in. 'What do they stand for?'

'Hail to thee, blithe spirit. Bird thou never wert —'

'You used the word bisbas,' the woman's voice broke in. 'What does that mean?'

'That from heaven or near it pourest thy full heart — '

'Are they initials? What do they stand for?'

'In profuse strains of un- of unpremeditated art.'

'You mentioned bisbas distinctly a few minutes ago,' the woman persisted in her level, unemotional voice. 'Now, are you going to tell me what it means or — '

'NO! WAIT! It means — Oh, what a rogue and peasant slave am I! I could a tale unfold whose lightest word would harrow up thy soul, freeze thy young blood, make thy two eyes like stars start from their spheres, thy knotted — '

'You're making this up,' the woman accused him. 'You still think this is a game?'

'Thy knotted and combined locks to part — '

The recitation was broken by a sound which made me rip the head-set off and push it at Tro.

'We've got to get in there. He must break soon.'

'Is that poetry he's quoting?' Tro, pale and strained, had been watching my face.

'Yes. Shakespeare, I think. Richie, we've got to get in there.'

'Easy, old Pat. We can't afford to go off at half cock again.'

Silently, Tro handed the head-set to Stan. She'd had enough.

A shadow crossed the window. Clement came in by the gaping door of the shed.

'Probe's through,' he whispered. 'Try the monitor now.'

Richie squatted down, shading a torch. He switched the set on. Immediately the small television screen lit up.

The fish-eye lens on the end of the hair-thin fibre-optic probe was peering into the room from high up on the wall. It relayed back a picture that was distorted like a reflection in a convex mirror. It showed a 120-degree arc of the inside of the room.

A man with a beard lay asleep on a couch. A second woman with blonde, cropped hair and a man with a moustache were sitting in chairs eating slices of bread and drinking coffee. One of them had a pad and pencil on his knee. There was a radio transceiver on a table by the chimney. No fire in the grate. Light came from two oil lamps on tables. It was just possible to see through the door of the kitchen. Beyond was another door which must lead to the cellar.

Clement squatted down to stare at the picture. Sound was also coming through the loudspeaker to the right of the screen, relayed by the spike mike, but reception was bad. The man and woman who were awake seemed to be discussing the text of the message they would send out on their next broadcast.

As we watched, the man with the moustache went over to the set, looking at his watch. It was 3 am. He pushed the aerial up the chimney, put on the head-set and picked up the mike.

He had his back to us as he operated the set. We could only hear a low murmur too indistinct for us to pick out any words.

A woman came up from the cellar and ran through the room, her hand to her mouth. She was heading for the bathroom but did not make it in time. She threw up in the corner of the room, to the fury of the others. Then she disappeared into the hall. She was a dark-haired vixen with her hair dragged back and tied in a pony-tail.

When the brief transmission ended the man turned back. The bearded one had wakened.

'It's confirmed. He says we're to shoot him at six. But we have to get the answers to those questions before then.'

'Oh, Christ! Haven't we done enough?'

'You know Federico,' the man with the moustache said.

Stan took the head-set off. 'They're giving him a rest but he's still babbling on.'

'The woman interrogator is being sick,' I explained.

'I'm not surprised. Intensive interrogation is unpleasant work.'

Tro looked at Stan oddly. Sympathy for the torturer was a new concept to her.

Clement said: 'Mustn't hurry this. Need a lot of time to plot their movements and routine.'

'Sod that!' I said. 'You haven't heard what's happening down in that cellar.'

'Pat's right,' Stan agreed. 'Man, we've got to put a stop to this.'

Tro said: 'Nobody should have to go through that.'

'Are you going to join us in the assault, Tro?' Clement asked.

Tro flared up at the implication.

'I bloody am! And I'm ready to go now without fart-arsing around about routine and movements.'

'Easy, now,' Richie warned. 'Keep your voices down. We'll go in when it's right to go in. We have to pick a moment when there's only one of them or better still nobody in the cellar.'

When Richie had outlined his plan for the break-in I went back to fetch the Saab. I took the brake off and let it run down

170

onto the flat ground clear of the trees. From there I had a clear run of a hundred yards to the wall of the chalet. The lounge was on this side.

'Suppose the Saab does not break the wall?' Clement had asked during the briefing.

'It will,' I'd answered with confidence. In fact I had no data to go on except vague memories of Saabs undergoing crash tests at the factory. When Clement had drilled the hole for the audio-visual probe he had discovered that there were two courses of bricks separated by a cavity filled with insulating foam. The extra weight of the bullet-proofing would make the Saab a formidable battering ram. I would be going in at the maximum speed I could achieve in reverse. That also was an unknown statistic and there was no scope for a trial run.

As I walked back to the shed the sky to eastward was slashed by lightning. After seconds the rumble of thunder echoed round the mountains. Another storm was lumbering towards us from the same stable as the first.

In the shed Richie had put on the head-set that was connected to the mike clamped to the wall above the cellar. At the same time he was watching the screen of the television monitor. Tro was staring at his face with an agonised expression, knowing all too well the kind of sounds he was hearing.

By the light of a shaded torch Clement and Stan were checking the Winchester pump-gun, the Ingram sub-machine guns, the Brownings and the stun grenades.

'They've broken him.' Richie did not take his eyes from the screen. There was only one terrorist in the visible sector. It was the bearded one. He was standing in front of the radio. 'He's telling them all about Bisbas and our nuclear release procedures — the lot. Now they're on about our contingency plans to counter an invasion through Poland. He hardly knows what he's saying. It's all mixed up with quotations from Shakespeare and poetry and stuff.'

'It's the sleep deprivation that's got to him more than the torture.' Clement was anxious to defend a fellow-soldier. 'He's beyond the limit. A man his age can't survive more than

171

five days without sleep.'

'Have they transmitted any information yet?'

'No. We've got to hit them before they do that. There's three of them down with him at the moment. I'm beginning to think one of them is a KGB agent. He's feeding questions to the woman interrogator, but I can't understand what he says.'

Richie took the head-phones off and handed them back to Tro. Reluctantly she put them on. Immediately her face winced and she bit hard on her lip.

'If two of them come up we go in at once, so let's make sure you all know what you've got to do. First of all code-names for our chums. Beardie and Moustache are easy. Brunette and Blondie for the women. The little KGB man is Ivan. Okay?'

Down in the cellar the interrogation was going well. Now that his resistance was broken the General had become like a child in the hands of his questioners. He still, out of habit, interjected lines of verse into his answers. The questioners steered him back to the subject with almost kindly patience. It was pathetic to listen to and also horrifying, for these revelations gave a glimpse of the holocaust that awaited the world if the fragile curtain of peace was ripped aside.

An hour dragged by. The storm came closer and closer till with a whoosh the rain swept down the hill. The huge drops drummed on the vestige of roof under which we were sheltering.

Tro kept looking at Richie, willing him to put a stop to the General's Calvary. But he would not budge while there were three terrorists down in the cellar.

It was sheer exhaustion, the body's craving for sleep, which at last brought the interrogation to an end. The General's voice grew weaker and slower. He made less and less sense. They threw buckets of water over him but he was out for the count.

'I think they're coming up!' Richie jumped to his feet. 'Grab your weapons and get to your positions. When I flash my torch once we go in. Okay, Clem?'

'Okay.'

I put on a pair of night goggles and went back to the Saab. I

172

had a Browning stuck into my waist-belt but my real weapon was the car. Before I reached the shelter of the front seat I was soaked. The rain was an ally. Its pounding on the roof of the chalet would provide noise cover.

There was no need this time to belt myself in. The engine started quietly on the automatic choke. I sat looking forward at my green-hued landscape. Everything was clearly visible as if lit by the glow from some hovering luminous spacecraft.

I saw Stan emerge from the shed with Tro. Each was holding an Ingram Mach 10 at waist level. They picked their way across the open ground to the chalet. With my night goggles on it was hard to believe they could not see more than the dim outline of the chalet's roof. Their hands were stretched out feeling for the brick wall. When they reached it they squatted down at either end under the broad overhang.

I knew that Richie was still in the shed watching the television monitor. He was waiting for the terrorists to come up from the cellar.

A minute passed before Clement came out of the shed. He was wearing the second pair of night goggles. The Browning which had become almost part of him was gripped in his right hand. Richie followed close behind, holding the back of Clement's jacket. He had the Winchester pump-gun in his free hand. They moved swiftly towards the house and stopped twenty feet from it. They were wearing the body-shield field jackets.

Richie turned. I saw his torch flash.

I let in the clutch. The car bounded forward, bucking as it gathered speed on the rough ground. A loud rattle came from beneath the body. The tyres were catapulting stones against the wheel arches.

At fifty feet from the house I flipped the car into a bootlegger turn and spun it through 180 degrees. Before she had completed the spin I was in reverse gear. The tail was now pointing at the wall of the house. The beam of Richie's torch was aimed at the point where I was to strike. I let in the clutch and floored the accelerator pedal.

The acceleration of the Turbo in reverse was phenomenal.

The low gear and high revs brought in the full boost of the compressor. When I was sure my aim was correct I faced the dashboard and pressed the back of my head hard against the head-rest. The car leaped and bounced as it flung itself at the wall.

The crash when it came was paralysing. I was slammed backwards by the brutal deceleration. The seat supports gave way under the gigantic force. I was jerked back onto the cushioned rear seat. The wall had been well and truly breached. Bricks thundered on the metal roof, mixed with the white gunge of the insulating material. The Saab had come to rest three quarters inside the room.

I gathered my wits and hauled myself up by the steering wheel. Through the side window I dimly saw two of the terrorists frozen into immobility by the shock.

Then came a mind-bending explosion. Clement had flung the first of his stun-grenades.

Two figures clawed their way in through the gap in the wall, slithering over the bonnet of the Saab, one on either side. The interior of the room was dark now. The explosion had blown the lamps off the tables. As he came level with me, Richie loosed off the pump-gun, spraying the room with shot. From my other side came the double detonation of Clement's Browning. I saw him dive into the room and go into a roll that carried him almost to the door leading to the kitchen. He bounced to his feet as he reached it. I saw him fling another grenade. As the concussion hit me he disappeared.

Three seconds had passed since my unlawful entry. Supporting myself by the steering wheel I restarted the stalled engine.

Richie had moved on towards the door that led to the hall. The Winchester boomed as he pumped it again. Stan had come in on the same side as Clement. His job was to follow Clement through to the cellar where the General was — just in case Clement got knocked out. But it was Stan who bought it.

He yelled and jerked as a bullet hit him, fired by someone lying on the ground. He slithered out of sight beside the Saab.

174

I rammed the gear lever into first and let in the clutch. The front wheels found a purchase on the fallen masonry and dragged the smashed rear of the car clear of debris. The boot lid had snapped open and was flapping like the wing of a wounded pheasant.

I nearly hit the figure standing outside. It was Tro. She was gripping the Ingram tight, nerving herself to go in and use it.

'There's one of them on the ground,' I yelled at her. 'He got Stan.'

She stepped towards the jagged opening. The terrorist on the ground got off one shot at her. Then she unleashed a two-second burst, the stubby Ingram remarkably steady in her hands. In that time the gun fired forty rounds into the room.

I had stopped the car and was getting out when the booming roar of the pump-gun came again from the far side of the house. I pulled the Browning out and went back to the gap in the ruined wall. One of the oil lamps crashing to the floor had ignited a curtain. The room was lit by the leaping orange flames.

Tro, horrified, was staring at what a burst of 9 mm parabellum ammo can do to a human body. Richie was lurching back through the door from the hall. Stan lay on the ground gasping. I turned him carefully on his side, put my finger in his mouth to make sure his tongue was not blocking the breathing passages.

'Three in here.' Richie was counting the bodies on the floor. 'I got Brunette coming out of the loo with her knickers in a twist. That leaves Ivan.'

'Stan!' My ringing ears could just hear Clement calling from the cellar. He needed his back-up man.

'Tro, look after Stan. Pat, you go to Clem. I'll stay up here in case anyone unexpected comes out of the woodwork.'

I pushed through the door into the kitchen. To the right another door opened onto stone stairs. I went down. The cellar was lit by an oil lamp that had weathered the blast. The smell of explosive and cordite hung in the air. Ivan lay on the floor. His ugly mouth was open in the rictus of death.

An iron bed, very similar to the one we had found in the

Vicolo Sant' Agnese, stood against the cellar wall. On it was stretched a human form. An extempore device for transmitting a variable electric current was on the table beside it — a twelve volt battery, an adjustable transformer, leads with bulldog clips on the end. An A4 notepad lay on the floor near Ivan.

The General had been stripped. He was still secured to the end of the bed-frame by a pair of handcuffs round each wrist. Blood was flowing from a wound in his chest.

'Ivan got a shot off before I could nail him. Things under control upstairs?'

'They're all dead. Stan stopped one. The place is on fire.'

The General's shirt lay on the floor. I picked it up. Luckily it was cotton, not nylon. I ripped one sleeve off and made it into a hard pad.

'Got to find the key to those cuffs.' Clement had knelt beside the KGB man and was searching his pockets.

I tore the body of the shirt into strips and knotted them together. Clement straightened up, cursing, and dashed up the stairs.

It was awkward working round the arms hand-cuffed to the bed, but I managed to tie my bandages so that the pad was pressed hard against the hole in the General's chest. The flow of blood was checked. There was no exit wound, so the bullet was still in him. His breathing was almost imperceptible but he was alive.

Clement came clattering back down the stairs.

'We can't find the key and there's no one left to ask. The room is becoming an inferno. We'll have to carry him out on the bed.'

'It won't fit through the door. Have to dismantle it.'

'Better be quick.' For once Clement was edgy.

The bed was of the simple design where the frame fits into four slots and holds the metal head and foot rigid. They're easy to dismantle — when you haven't got a body lying on them. I got Clement to take the weight of the frame while I hammered the head out of its sockets. Then we dragged the bed-head across the floor and up the stairs. Attached by the wrists the General came with it. It was rough treatment for his trailing legs but the area of the wound was protected.

There was a dodgy moment when we nearly got stuck in the doorway at the top. We met Richie in the kitchen. He had found cloths and soaked them in water. The house was now full of smoke. Clement and I were already choking. The pine panelling of the sitting-room had ignited and was burning fiercely. The heat had set fire to the chairs in the middle of the room. They had exploded into flame.

Richie had tied a wet cloth over his mouth and nose. He flung one each to Clement and me. We knotted them behind our heads. Richie ripped a curtain from the window, dunked it in the sink and draped it over the General's naked body so that it covered his face.

Then Clement and I picked him up, complete with bed-head, and bore him through the blazing room to the gap in the wall. We carried him twenty yards clear of the building before we set him down.

'Where's Richie?'

'He's still in there.'

Clement was starting back towards the chalet when an apocalyptic figure came staggering out. Richie was clutching the A4 pad on which the interrogators had made their notes of the General's revelations. His face was blackened with smoke and his luxuriant eyebrows had gone.

Stan was lying on the ground with Tro kneeling beside him. She was still shaking from reaction after killing a man.

'He's got a bullet in his lower gut. It went under the flak waistcoat. I've put a dressing on it but it's, you know, very temporary. I mean, he ought to be in intensive care.'

We all shed some clothes to cover the General. At least it had stopped raining but at this altitude the morning was chill. The burning house radiated heat, warming one side of our bodies. It was flaming like a torch. The whole Piano and the woods behind were lit by the yellowish glow. The good people of Capretto would soon be hurrying up to investigate what they must believe to be a case of spontaneous combustion.

To the east, low down under the departing storm clouds, the sky was already lightening.

I rummaged among the tools in the crushed boot of the Saab till I found a hacksaw. I used it to cut through the handcuffs on the General's wrists. After that we were able to make him marginally more comfortable. He had half recovered consciousness. He still thought he was in the hands of his captors and was spouting verse, going on about "to hear the lark begin his flight and singing startle the dull night from his watch-tower in the skies".

Richie and Clement had been watching me, talking. Now Richie came and stooped beside me.

'Pat, old pal. You've flown helicopters, haven't you?'

'I flew a Hiller. Years ago.'

'Could you fly a Jet-Ranger?'

TEN

The problem about flying a strange helicopter is how to start it. The old Hillers I'd flown were piston-engined. The Jet-Ranger was powered by a turbine. As a plate inside the cockpit told me the power plant was an Alison 250-C20 developing 317 shaft horse power. The fuel gauge showed that the tank was less than half full. The big snag was that its passenger capacity was limited to five. There were now six of us.

The others had helped me to push the Jet-Ranger on its dolly wheels out of the shed. I had shooed them all away while I sat in the pilot's seat and communed with the mass of instruments before me. They filled not only the instrument panel but part of the roof over my head.

I was familiar enough with the workings of a turbine to know what the probable sequence would be. After five minutes study of the panel and a search into my memory I was ready to have a go.

The first move was easy. I'd found a switch marked START. I turned it and had the satisfaction of hearing an electric motor start up and then a whining sound which gradually built up. That meant the compressor turbine was accelerating. I made a second switch to introduce fuel to the combustion chamber. The compressor dial had risen to 25,000 rpm.

Still praying, I made a third switch which I hoped would ignite the mixture. The result was impressive. The engine accelerated up to governed rpm, about 80,000 revs per minute. Above me the rotors started to turn. Hastily I searched the cockpit for the rotor brake to make sure it was off.

The engine was now self-sustaining, or, in layman's language, automatic. A computer would keep it in its

179

governed rpm range. I was ready to try and fly it.

Over on the other side of the Piano the roof of the villa had fallen in. Flames and sparks were sucked upwards by the draught. A pillar of smoke rose high into the rapidly lightening sky.

As soon as they'd seen the rotors begin to turn Richie, Clement and Tro started to carry the General over to the Jet-Ranger. Together we eased him onto the rear passenger seat. Then they brought Stan and laid him on the floor where the passengers' feet would normally be.

It was going to be a tight fit. When the load is too heavy for a car she goes down on her springs. With a helicopter the results are less predictable.

Richie and Clement were arguing about which of them would stay behind so as not to exceed the maximum load.

'Get aboard,' I told them. 'The fuel tank is half empty. We can make it.'

The three of them scrambled in. Richie sat beside me. The suitcase containing the billion lire was stowed behind the rear seat. Clement and Tro squatted between the seats. She was still pale and subject to bouts of the shivers. I reached over and closed the door.

'You know what you're doing, old Pat?'

'Soon find out.'

I had my right hand on the cyclic control, the column between my legs. My left was on the collective pitch lever. I pulled the collective up, up, up. The Jet-Ranger rose from the ground.

'Cheers,' said Richie.

Twenty feet up I pushed the cyclic forward. The Jet-Ranger immediately accelerated, at the same time sinking rapidly towards the ground. I kept the power on. With an increase in forward speed she might gain lift from the air flow. She bounced twice before we reached the edge of the Piano. We went over with a downward swoop. But now the increased speed was giving us lift. I eased back on the cyclic. We rose majestically into the air.

Clement and Tro were picking themselves off the floor.

180

I said: 'Piece of cake. I've got her now.'

Richie was silent, unusual for him.

Now that I had gained altitude and was adjusting to the feel of the aircraft it was easy. I was sure I could get her down somehow.

Up here we had come into the rays of the rising sun. The panorama through the curved perspex windshield was glorious. Below us the Appenines were sharply etched by the low sun. The mountains cast deep shadows in all the valleys. To the east I could see the ribbon of the autostrada snaking across viaducts and disappearing into tunnels. The blazing house far below had diminished to the scale of a garden bonfire.

I was heading south, looking for Florence. If my calculations were correct it was about fifteen minutes flying time away.

The first indication that I was on course was a crenellated sixteenth century tower protruding from the morning mist that lay over the plain. Near it rose the familiar dome of the cathedral with Giotto's square tower adjoining it.

Behind me the General was still muttering incoherently. Stan was unconscious, his breathing a raucous snore. The others were silent. I could not tell whether they were praying for happy landings or moved to awe by the beauty of the city below, bathed in the light which had inspired Beato Angelico.

'I'm going to dump her down in the Piazza Signoria. Okay?'

No one answered. I veered towards the east so as to come in against the wind. That would mean passing perilously close to the Cinquecento tower. The approach would not be as shallow as I'd like.

'Mask your faces everybody.' Richie had found his voice. 'When we land — Correction. *If* we land, nobody say anything. Pat, you tell them we're NOCS. As soon as we know the General and Stan are in care we go our ways and meet up at the British Consulate.'

The central square of Florence was coming up to meet us fast. At this hour of the morning there were few people about.

They began to scatter as they realised that the helicopter was going to land. The unashamedly naked statues posing outside the Uffizi Gallery remained totally indifferent to the *commedia*.

The tower slid past on my left, very close. With my two feet on the pedals controlling the tail rotor I tried to yaw the aircraft into the wind but I was losing height too fast. The cobbled surface of the square rushed up. We landed like a splay-footed duck hitting the water.

I left the rotors turning, opened the door and stepped down. A *vigile urbano*, resplendent in white uniform, helmet and all the trimmings, was marching towards me. The expression on his face was one of outrage.

'*Attenzione*!' I shouted at him in Italian. 'The rotors!'

He stopped dead, instinctively ducking. I followed up the advantage.

'We're NOCS,' I rapped at him.

'NOCS?' His mouth dropped open. NOCS was a household word in Italy, as emotive as SAS in Britain.

'We have the *Generalissimo*. He is badly wounded. Send for an ambulance at once.'

Behind me Richie, Clement and Tro had climbed out, each holding a gun. Richie had his precious suitcase in his left hand. Businesslike with their masked faces, they formed a little crescent facing the small crowd. Awed, the people kept their distance beyond the sweep of the rotors. As the word spread more and more Florentines came running. The *vigile* had hurried to a police telephone at the side of the square. He was talking fast into the instrument.

I saw now that Piazza Signoria was decked with flags and bunting. A small grandstand had been erected at one end. Today must be some kind of *festa*.

Within minutes I heard the ambulance siren, wailing on a slowly rising and falling note. It grew louder and louder till the white vehicle burst into the square. The *vigile* had been joined by a colleague. The two cops parted the crowd to let it through.

The ambulance backed up as close as possible to the Jet-

Ranger. Two attendants leaped out. The second *vigile*, more officious than the first, had taken charge. He gestured the ambulance men towards the helicopter. They ducked under the rotors and went aboard to examine the two prone bodies.

I strolled over to the driver's door.

'What hospital are you from?'

'Arcispedale Santa Maria Nuova.'

The attendants had lifted Stan and the General out on stretcher-slings. With speed and efficiency they transferred them to the stretchers which would slide into the ambulance.

'Scatter,' Richie said in a low but clear voice.

While everyone's eyes were on the two bodies being carefully loaded into the ambulance, the four of us moved into the crowd, each one heading in a different direction.

The British Consulate was on the Lungarno Corsini only five hundred metres from Piazza Signoria. I was the first to arrive. A broad archway led through to an inner courtyard. The Italian concierge at the entrance explained that the Consulate was on the first floor of the building. Not surprisingly the offices were not open at a quarter to seven in the morning. None of the staff lived on the premises.

'*Oggi festa*,' he told me, grinning.

I asked him to 'phone through to the Consul. No dice. With my smoke-blackened face, singed hair and a shirt that had dried on my body I probably looked like one of those drug addicts who congregate on the steps of Florence's cathedral.

After a lot of persuasion he agreed to telephone the duty secretary. He had the number in case of emergencies. After a great many apologies for disturbing the secretary, he handed me the 'phone.

The voice was female. The lady was a little displeased at such an early call. She was probably sick and tired of dealing with British junkies who had run out of money.

'This is an emergency,' I said. 'I really need to speak to the Consul —'

'The Consul is away at a conference. In any case, we —'

'Can you get down here? It's really urgent.'

183

'The office does not open till — '

'Listen. I can't say too much on the 'phone. You've heard of General Stewart?'

A short silence. Then: 'Are you — Who are you?'

To stir her into action I said: 'I'm acting for COBRA — the Cabinet Office Briefing Room. This is a matter involving national security. Now, can you — '

She had already made up her mind. 'I'll come down right away. It'll take me about ten minutes.'

The concierge was looking at me with greater respect as I hung up the receiver.

'Is there a waiting-room anywhere?'

'*Sisignore. Venga. Venga pure.*'

He was about to show me up to the first floor when Richie appeared at the entrance. He was still lugging his suitcase. Usually immaculate in his turnout he was now a right mess. His face was even more smoke-blackened than mine. The eyebrows which normally curled over his forehead had vanished and his face looked strangely naked. His shirt was in tatters and one trouser leg torn. His blond hair was wild and his glass eye gleamed wickedly.

We both followed the concierge up to the first floor. He opened the door of a waiting-room, his veiled eyes stealing surreptitious glances at us. We walked into a room furnished with such elegance that we hesitated to soil the chairs with our foul-smelling clothes.

During the quarter of an hour before the secretary arrived Clement and Tro were shown in by the now completely mystified concierge. None of us said much. We were still in the shocked state that follows intensive action and danger. We were probably sharing the same thought. Of the eight who had assembled in Richie's flat five mornings ago we four were the only survivors. Nick, Franco and Johnnie were dead. Stan had no more than a fifty-fifty chance of pulling through.

Richie put the suitcase flat on the Persian rug and opened the catches.

'We don't know how all this is going to work out, so you'd better each take a wad.'

He handed each of us a bundle containing a thousand of the 100,000 lire notes.

'That's not as much as it looks. Only about five grand.'

We just had time to stash our wads away before the door opened. A comely woman of about thirty-five put her head in. She was comfortingly British and competent.

She blinked a few times when she saw the four dishevelled characters waiting for her.

'Good heavens! Didn't you say — Look here, is this some kind of leg-pull?'

Richie stood up. Even now he was an imposing figure.

'No leg-pull. You're in the picture about General Stewart, of course?'

'Yes.' She came into the room and leaned her back against the door. 'Lady Stewart arrived here only last night — '

'*What?*'

'Yes.' The secretary searched Richie's and my face. We'd both exclaimed together. 'She said she had information that her husband was somewhere in the mountains north of Florence. She wanted us to — '

'Well, I'll be stuffed and roasted! Where is she now?'

'The Vice-Consul took her back to his home. She's in a bit of a state, actually — '

'That's very convenient.' Richie's face creased in a broad grin. 'It so happens that we've just landed her husband in Piazza Signoria.'

It was an hour before the Vice-Consul arrived with Lady Stewart. We made use of the waiting period by cleaning ourselves in the Consulate's washrooms and consuming the coffee and rolls which Miss Willoughby had made the concierge fetch from a nearby café.

When Lady Stewart burst into the Consul's office, where we were now waiting, she was hardly recognisable as the carefully self-controlled woman we had first seen in Brown's Hotel. Uncertainty, lack of sleep, hope deferred, had carved deep lines on her face. Her eyes had withdrawn into dark hollows. She had dressed in haste and her clothes were all

185

askew.

She homed on Tro as soon as she saw her. 'Is it true? Is it true that you've brought him back?'

'Yes. It's true.'

'Where — where is he?'

She stared round her as if she expected the General to rise smiling from one of the chairs.

'They've taken him to the hospital of Santa Maria Nuova.'

Lady Stewart's eyes widened and her hand flew to her throat. 'He's not — Had they done terrible things to him?'

Richie, Clement and I exchanged a glance. It was a silent vow that none of us would ever tell that the General had been broken.

'He's in intensive care,' Tro said. 'He has a bullet wound, but he's going to be all right.' Then Tro's curiosity got the better of her. 'Lady Stewart, how did you get here? We thought we'd lost you when you fell for that con trick and went to Piazza Colonna.'

'It wasn't a trick, my dear.' The flicker of a smile eased the tension on Lady Stewart's face. 'It was a peasant, a moss-gatherer from the mountains. He came all the way to Rome to find me. He'd been a prisoner of war in England and was very pro-British. Poor man, he was as terrified of the police as of the terrorists. I had to promise — '

The Vice-Consul had followed Lady Stewart into the room. He was a portly man of about fifty, the kind you'd expect to meet on the first tee at Wentworth golf course on a Sunday morning. The grey suit was obviously London-tailored.

'Santa Maria Nuova is only a quarter of a mile from here, Lady Stewart. I'll have my driver take you round there at once.'

'How very kind.'

She was at the door when she remembered us. Richie, Clement, Tro and I were standing awkwardly in a half circle.

'Forgive me.' She came back towards us. 'I nearly forgot the most important thing.'

She stood looking at us. Gratitude is most eloquent when it can find no words to express itself. Her glistening eyes said it

186

all. Realising that her throat and tongue were on strike she came and embraced each one of us, Tro last of all.

Then she turned to the waiting Miss Willoughby and without a word went out of the room.

When she had gone Richie cleared his throat and went to the window overlooking the inner courtyard. Tro was blowing her nose. Myself, I felt a painful sense of emptiness. At this moment it was impossible to contemplate any future.

The telephone ringing on the Consul's desk cut into the silence. The Vice-Consul went round to pick it up.

'British Consulate . . . Yes, speaking . . . Oh, good morning, sir . . . Yes, it's quite true. Can you hold one moment, sir?'

He held the receiver away from his ear and raised his eyebrows at us.

'It's the Ambassador — from Rome. Er — do you mind?'

He gestured towards a door beside the indispensable portrait of Her Majesty Queen Elizabeth II. We took the hint and went through to the ante-room.

Four minutes later he called us back in again. He was obviously relieved, a man from whose back a great weight had been lifted. Now that he knew he was going to be rid of us he could afford to be expansive.

'Well, it's all fixed up.' His manner was almost friendly. 'We've made a deal with the Italians. They've agreed to turn a blind eye to everything. The official version will be that the rescue operation was carried out by the NOCS. They'll get the credit, naturally.'

The Vice-Consul moved behind his desk, unconsciously underlining the fact that we had ceased to be his responsibility.

'There are conditions, of course. You are to say nothing about all this, not now or ever. And you have to be out of Italy by tonight.'

'No problem,' Richie said.

Staff were arriving and the consular offices were opening as we went down the monumental stairway to the courtyard. At

187

the entrance to the archway a small queue of harassed British tourists were waiting to unload their problems on the Consulate officials.

We walked out into the sunlight of the Lungarno. I felt a touch on my forearm. It was Tro, putting her arm in mine. I looked down into her face with surprise.

'Patrick.'

'Yes.'

'You remember? I mean, after we put the Maserati in the field?'

I was not likely to forget that torrid kiss on the road from Capretto.

'Do you think we could — ?' For once Tro was fumbling for words. 'For some reason I've started to feel, you know, sort of randy. It's crazy, isn't it?'

'Natural reaction. After what we did up at the chalet.'

'The thing is — ' The hand took a firmer hold on my arm. 'I mean, can we do something about it?'

Richie and Clement were walking on ahead, Richie carrying his now much lighter suitcase. They were arguing amicably about the rival merits of Brownings and Ingrams for close encounters.

'The Excelsior Italia is the top hotel in Florence,' I said. 'It's about two hundred yards back up the Lungarno.'

With a hundred million lire stuffed into various pockets I could afford to lash out. Our fingers interlaced. My pulses were already racing.

'Let's turn back,' she said. I felt her start to tremble. 'But we go Dutch. Okay?'